Th.
ma
lon
anot
mad.
numl

Oper

ABSOLUTION

Absolution

A mystery by

Anthony Shaffer

SEVERN HOUSE

This first U.K. hardback edition published 1979 by
SEVERN HOUSE PUBLISHERS LTD, of
144–146 New Bond Street, London W1Y 9FD
with grateful acknowledgement to Transworld Publishers Ltd

ISBN 0 7278 0544 4

Shaffer, Anthony
  Absolution.
  I. Title
  823'.9'1F   PR6069.H258A/

  ISBN 0-7278-0544-4

Printed in Great Britain by The Anchor Press Ltd
and bound by Wm Brendon & Son Ltd
both of Tiptree, Essex

And what rough beast, its hour come round at last, slouches towards Bethlehem to be born.

CONTENTS

Part One

TWO KINGDOMS

If you or I were to contemplate putting a man into Hell, where would we begin? Begin with his belief in the existence of such a place. Father Goddard believed in Hell! Also helpful was his unwavering belief in an alternative to that place, he was certain he eventually would find himself. But while Father Goddard's sights were fixed on Heaven, the only reality, an implacable force had guided him away from the Light and into a realm of the deepest darkness. Imagine then his despair when he found his journey ended in Hell ... and that one of his brightest pupils was the Shade who had charted his descent.

There is a certain madness that descends on the dormitories and corridors of large boarding schools at the end of the summer term, and St Anthony's College, Sommerbury, is no exception. With the examinations tackled and presented for evaluation, there are eight school days to fill before the major summer holiday empties the old manor house of its human contents. In this period the timetable of formal lessons is adjusted to morning work only, leaving the afternoons free for masters to correct papers and prepare reports. However, for the boys, these days are a whirl of activity. Inter-house debates, form tennis challenges, staff–student cricket, chess tournaments; the feature event being a production of some play or operetta by the drama and music society. Extra-curricular activities on such a programmed scale were a considered innovation to keep the five hundred boys fully supervised and occupied, having regard to the events of the previous year. For, in the old days (which in school chronology includes last year), the fever of term-ending had often taken the form of various practical jokes, usually designed and executed by final year students.

These great larks ranged from harmless and infantile sprees

of short-sheeting beds to dangerous acts of sabotage. Like the case of the chapel bells.

This most famous of larks was legendary among students for its bravura and daring, notorious with the staff for its costly destructiveness, memorable for all who experienced it. The inspired exhibitionist was never identified despite an investigation to discover his identity rivalling the Spanish Inquisition in unpleasant thoroughness. The trickster or, more likely, tricksters were specialists in applied physics. They had devised a system to interweave the chapel bell-ropes, then hang them with weights from the gym in such a way that the bells continued to ring without handling. Any movement of one rope to stop the cacophony increased the downweight on another. So the noise continued unabated for nearly an hour. The vibration in the old chapel was so violent that four statuettes of saints were dislodged from their niches above the choir-stand. This year only two of them had been replaced as the Holy See had decanonised their fallen brothers; a fortunate economy, in retrospect, though at the time the disgraceful incident had been seen as an act of vulgar hooliganism.

Moreover, Father Goddard, the newly appointed deputy principal, had seen it as a rebellious affront to his authority. This foretaste of the apocalypse was an ideal opportunity to consolidate his power. The bell ropes had been cut and the wild bells silenced. He had then assembled the whole school in the chapel with the severed ropes and the shattered saints and demanded that those responsible for this outrage have the courage of their convictions. Let the culprits name themselves and accept their punishment. There had been no response. He had waited calmly, at last daring the ringleader to step forward. The unintentional pun had been met with peals of laughter, which broke the awed silence of the assembled boys so that Goddard had been forced to treat the misdemeanour as a personal insult. He had equated the incident with sin, and, as sin was a personal affront to Christ in the realm of the spirit, this behaviour was a despicable wound to himself and an act of base ingratitude to the school. An emotive attack on the twelve senior boys to whom eventually he had intuitively ascribed authorship of the crime, was a simple matter of calculation which achieved the desired effect, for all of them had an affection for him. One boy made the fatal mistake of trying to explain that it had not been personally meant against Goddard, God, or Jesus. He had dismissed him with a silent wave of his hand. Then one by one, the twelve boys had been lashed with occasional wit and bludgeoned with bruising sarcasm for over the years he had come to know them, their secret aspirations, their fears, and, most importantly, their varying degrees of vulnerability.

First he had named them and elevated them; then inch by inch degraded them and buried them, bleeding, in the graveyard of their fellows' contempt. The lesson had been witnessed by the present school, and was never forgotten. The 'Bell Lark' had entered legend, the last of its species. Father Goddard assumed an awesome reputation as the scourge of Sommerbury, a veritable Hound of God.

On this afternoon, a year later, that same hound sat in his study doggedly applying himself to another task of correction —his form's examination papers.

As an English master of the college, he was required to supervise all the examination work in that subject. As a form master he was required to oversee all the answers his own form had given, even in subjects he did not teach where the marking had already been done by others.

Arthur Dyson's effort was the first on the block. Arthur had chosen the question about symbols in King Lear. After one paragraph of unintelligible drivel, Goddard decided he would sooner be deafened by another prank with the bells than rattled by the clash of symbols in Dyson's lame analysis of the play. However, he persevered to the end, begrudgingly wrote that the basic ideas were good but the whole essay lacked presentation, passed him, but marked him low. 51.

Benjamin Stanfield's essay was next. Beautifully presented. A cogent and imaginative piece of work. 'Perhaps you dwell too much on the scenes of cruelty'; he wrote in the margin. 'I don't care to be reminded of them, Benji. Otherwise well done. 85.'

Sackville and Hardy had chosen the alternative question— a rather factual dissertation on the effect of the Age of Revolutions on English Literature with particular attention to the Romantics. He corrected them easily. Mostly straightforward regurgitation of his various lectures. Nothing inept, nothing brilliant. After ten or so papers his head began to ache and his writing hand deaden. Within two hours he had completed his form's papers and decided to check through some of the others. As he suspected, they revealed themselves to be more instruments of torture. Illegible handwriting was bad enough. Relentlessly poor grammar was excruciating. The *Peine Forte et Dure* of them all was atrocious spelling. After suffering six thousand words of this at various hands, crying 'no more', with a flourish of red pencil he cut a remark into the margin of Rowland's essay. He turned his back on the remaining stacks of answers in favour of a walk around the college.

Father Roberts was the only person in the whole dorm area.

'I'm all finished, Father. Here is your form's Chemistry to look at. All are corrected. On the whole, not bad, this term.'

Goddard nodded distractedly, as he walked on. 'Put them inside with the rest,' he shouted, 'I'm just going to take a walk to clear my head. The effects of the French Revolution may have nourished the imagination of Keats and Shelley, but in my case, a migraine is about all it's inspired.'

Summer was slow in coming this year. The days remained cold, the hours damp and the evenings misty.

Basket Wood, on the Sommerbury Estate, though well-populated with trees, looked especially stark with so many dead and dying elms. One mournful cluster of them on a ridge was made even more pathetic by a fresh and flowering alien in their midst, impatient at summer's delay. A gang of rooks riding over these elms to their tattered nests made a sinister backdrop to Sommerbury in the sunless mid-afternoon.

The brisk walk across the ordered grounds had cleared Father Goddard's head. He stood at the very edge of the fields with his back to the manor house and adjacent buildings, like the celebrant before an ornate altar-piece set on a terraced green knoll. Before him lay the disordered congregation of woodlands, and the river. The tock of batting, vague burr of fielding, briefly diverted his attention to the cricket match, set not so incongruously as it might seem at the right hand of the sanctuary (the wicket does make a Holy Trinity and the red ball the devil).

'Good ball, Roehampton . . .' intoned Father Gladstone. As

a fielder in white ran in pursuit to the boundary. Goddard's gaze returned to the woodscape. As a young missionary teacher in Africa he used to stand at the clearing's edge facing the obscuring tangle of green. There, in those younger days, imagination would run wildly from sound to shadow, invoking the most pagan enemies who had prepared for him a glorious martyrdom. The only virulent enemy he found there was the malaria which forced him back to England.

He laughed quietly at himself—a very rare event nowadays. The uprush of the old fear of the disordered forest, after all these years, certainly warranted it. He became pensive again. What on earth could have awakened those thoughts? Most likely Benjamin Stanfield's superb essay.

Benji showed promise of real brilliance in the question on Lear. Well, at least the first part was brilliant (where he explored the blinding of Gloucester). Benji argued this was a central image of the play's recurring symbol of blindness. Most of the action arose from the suffering caused by varying conditions of blindness. After the suffering, a truthful vision could be realized. An elegant proposition, spoiled only by the cold medical detail which described at length the exact procedure of the cruel plucking out of the man's eyes.

In the second section of the essay Benji made too much of the role of Edgar. Goddard dismissed this overemphasis as Benji's passion to play that particular part. There was a wildness in Benji that was fascinated by all that Mad Tom disguise ... all that ranting naked in the rain.

Goddard remembered he should drop in and see how rehearsals for the theatrical venture were progressing. 'Patience' by Gilbert and Sullivan was this term's offering. He turned away from the wood and made towards the buildings.

This past year he had so consolidated his position as deputy principal that, despite the title, he was the man in charge. Failing health had removed Father Rivers (Old Man Rivers in the *lingua franca* of the dorm) further from the scene. The other deputy principal, Father Moore, was a Goddard appointee who posed no real threat to his eventual elevation.

Moore, a bland accountant type, ten years younger than Goddard, was nervously efficient at the time-consuming duties of fundraising, records, and the endless logistics of timetabling. He was ideal for the role of Administrator and Bursar. Goddard was well rid of those problems. His main brief was the academic and spiritual life of the school. With the paperwork firmly on Moore's rounded shoulders, he could keep close contact with the boys—his daily bread. He had retained his status as English subject master for all forms, but contrary to usual practice he remained a form master, domiciled in the small study-bedroom adjoining the dormitory of his senior class. Moving away from the heart of the school to a large private suite in the administration wing was an isolation he could not afford.

One considerable adjustment to his workload (which did conform with correct practice for a priest in his position) was to cease hearing weekly confessions. Instead, he appointed two other priests as chaplains to the whole school. His role as spiritual adviser had its finest expression on Sundays at the main nine o'clock mass. He celebrated, served by a team of altar-boys selected from his own house, the 'God Squad' as the chosen few were jocularly known. The chief altar-boy was Benjamin Stanfield.

Despite his authoritarian reputation, Goddard enjoyed a good measure of popularity among staff and students alike. They respected his ceaseless dedication. Though his manner was at times difficult, he was, on most occasions, charming if without warmth, tolerant if without compassion. Like many men in the middle of middle age, he had become a surplus heart, pride its blood and vanity its blindness.

Outwardly he seemed the paragon of success. He was still quite handsome in a lean ascetic way. Beneath the auburn hair, bright snow-white at the temples, was a strong-boned face on which time was only beginning its final sculpturing. Unlike the saints in the chapel, whom the centuries had blown into featureless oblivion, this face had marked character. In fact, in moments of determination and shows of will, it was impregnable as a granite fortress, the penetrating grey eyes, vigilant watchmen to ward off any advances into the heart of its keeper—Goddard's heart, a God-forsaken place.

As a young priest, he had been considered the ideal Catholic teacher of young men—athletic, ascetic and intellectual—'a vigorous mind and body wherein burns spiritual fire'. The years since his return from Africa had somewhat changed that ideal. Occasionally, as in the case of Benjamin, he saw the

glorious possible restated. For Benji represented a rich re-
source for the soldiery of Jesus, to reinforce his own fight
against atheism and its cohorts—the mindless materialism of
a post-war Britain devoid of moral structure, manifested in the
cultural and political impotence of society. A society whose
spiritual centre was without positive energy.

Goddard, unlike many of his generation of Jesuits, was
not a socialist but framed a vision peculiarly his own. The
Goddardists were to be the grand viziers of the new society,
warrior-priests guiding the captains of its endeavour. He was
ambitious for all the boys in his God Squad. With his blessing
they would leave Sommerbury for university and, God willing,
the seminary, better armed to combat the world's miseries than
boys from other institutions. For them the experience at
Sommerbury would be synonymous with the experience of
Goddard.

His teaching, his personality, even his mannerisms were the
mysterious stigmata on the lives of those boys who came within the range of his vision. In fact, within a couple of decades
these, his sons, would bear him tribute when they presented
their own sons into his keeping, according to plan.

His walk had now brought him to the main quadrangle. To
his right was the chapel, to his left, the assembly hall where
'Patience' was in frenetic last minute rehearsal for that evening.
He was heading in that direction but changed his mind, de-
ciding instead that a visit to the chapel for a few moments of
prayer would be fitting. He was always encouraging the boys
to make at least one such visit each day.

Father Pollard, an old priest, was placing roses from the
garden at the feet of St Anthony's statue. 'Afternoon, God
bless,' he mouthed across the chapel. Goddard inclined his
head in reply.

The evening prayer began.

> The Lord is kind and full of compassion.
> Slow to anger, abounding in love.
> How good is the Lord to all,
> Compassionate to all his creatures ...

The chapel was the oldest part of the manor. The original
place of worship for the monastery, it had stood since Anglo-

Saxon times, though the structure itself was Gothic, nineteenth century. By the reign of Henry the Eighth, this particular monastic house had grown rich and powerful. During the dissolution of the monasteries, house and estates had passed into the possession of the newly-created Earls of Sommerbury. The order of monks thus dispossessed had placed a curse on the head of the family, that each owner should die without an heir. Over the years, the Sommerbury family were hard-pressed but, despite the childless marriages, kept the property until the early twenties. The last Earl died childless. The house and estate fell vacant. The sole relative of the final Earl was Professor Percival Lacey-Bourne. He was, by chance or heavenly design, a convert to Catholicism and, like most new converts, more Catholic than those to the manner born. More faithful, more hopeful, and in this case, most charitable.

The devout old scholar presented Sommerbury to the Jesuits for the establishment of a school. Such beneficence would surely secure him a front row seat at the Day of Judgement and redress the wrong of his ancestors. Sommerbury House became St Anthony's College, Sommerbury, whilst the main boarding section was blessed with his name—Lacey Hall.

Goddard often told the school story to parents after tea, taking great delight in playing on the irony of the inherent curse, which was still in effect. For the owners were Fathers who as priests perforce were childless. He was always careful to add that this was merely a folk tale, not real evidence of the workings of the Almighty. Superstition was an aspect of religion far too subjective and vague for his taste. Though he did indulge dear old Father Pollard, who would proffer this fairy-tale to the first year intake as an example of God's partiality to English Catholicism.

> The eyes of all creatures look to you
> And you give them their food in due time
> You open wide your hand—
> Grant the desires of all who live ...

His prayer ended, 'And I will give you glory, Oh God, my King,' with a genuflection in the aisle. The sun was out. A stream of light was breathing life through a stained glass window depicting the Slaughter of Innocents.

Goddard mused that Herod slaying the first-born would provide an apposite reference to the curse when next he told the anecdote. That was his style. He knew how to manipulate his audience. The more he insisted the tale was fiction, the more he would subtly counter his own argument, spicing the narrative with palatable evidence to the contrary. The more he pressed his disbelief in it, the more his listeners desired for it to be true. Sometimes an eager listener would quote a piece of Goddard's evidence as conclusive proof of the story's veracity, to which he would reply with cunning astonishment that he had not really looked at it from that perspective . . .

In the final analysis, Sommerbury and its colourful heritage were an ideal setting for a middle-sized boarding school. There was ample room for community work, and enough corners and corridors for privacy when needed.

Goddard passed down the corridor on his way to the dress rehearsal. As he did, boys lounging there sprang to their feet. Such was the ritual when a ranking priest came into close proximity. If he was merely passing, the greeting 'Good afternoon, Father,' was sufficient. Should the priest have occasion to address the boy, the response was then, 'Good afternoon, Father, God bless you.' These greetings rippled down the hall in Goddard's wake. He replied to most with a nod and a half-smile, but occasionally . . .

'Simpson. Straighten your tie. You look like a lout.' A group of Dragoons from 'Patience' stopped fighting among themselves immediately as he swung into the hall.

In there, chaos reigned under the direction of Father Henry, the music master: lights were being hung, backcloths painted, seats being placed in position in the main body of the hall. The orchestra of boys were playing the prelude to Lady Jane's Aria. Father Henry, backing down the hall to greet Goddard, stood on Graham Logan's fingers.

'Graham, please move into the side room with those programmes. Down One please.'

All lights fell to near-blackout. 'One! One!'

The lights brightened abruptly to a dazzle. A disembodied voice called from somewhere behind the proscenium, 'It keeps sticking, Father.'

'I'll have a look at it Father. I'm rather good at electrics,' cried Lady Jane.

'Arthur! Remain seated and sing, please. Take it from ...'

'Reduced with rouge ... Father,' called the boy conductor.

'Thank you, Reiner. Arthur ... "Reduced with rouge".'

Goddard loathed Gilbert and Sullivan as poor men's classical music. It was an affront to the intelligence and, when performed by an all male cast, verged on the obscene. When Father Henry greeted him, his dislike of the piece was immediately made plain.

'But Father,' explained Henry, 'it does provide a large cast for all the willing participants—*Pink* gels on Arthur, not steel grey. Come along fellows, use your imagination, she's a romantic lead ... Lady Jane, not Lady Macbeth!'

The lights continued to fluctuate, steel grey gels fluttering into straws and pinks. Goddard's gaze settled on Lady Jane, a seated figure in a tatty mauve dress, a cello between her legs. She was made even more grotesque by the uncompromising steel light and the lead-white make-up Arthur had chosen to give her face.

'A little too much rouge on the cheeks, I should think. The words say enough without the warpaint,' commented Goddard.

'Well, Father, the correct lighting will soften the image ... watch the tempo, Arthur ... Lah, Lah ... don't race ahead of the orchestra.'

Arthur stood up. Father Henry signalled him down. In standing, Arthur glimpsed the other priest. It could only be Father Goddard he quickly realized. He immediately launched himself back into the aria, rounding the vowels and generally overdoing the characterisation for Goddard's benefit.

> 'Silvered is the raven hair
> Spreading is the parting straight ...'

The dragoons in the wings fell about with laughter at the excessive display.

> 'Mottled the complexion fair
> Halting is the youthful gait
> Hollow is the laughter free
> Spectacled the limpid eye ...'

This whole display only reinforced Goddard's disgust at the inappropriateness of both play and casting. Father Henry was nodding with delight.

'I must say our Lady Jane is coming along well—she'll be quite a hit tonight.'

'Rather bold casting,' replied Goddard. 'Dyson is a surprising choice.'

Father Henry disliked Goddard's tone. He knew he was not particularly fond of Arthur.

'Well, yes, Father ... his slight impediment does limit his movement, but the dress covers his brace. He is very good vocally, very clever, in fact—Mackintosh—Forbes, too much noise in the wings. Have a little respect for your fellow artists.'

Henry moved away from Goddard to have another look at the lighting board, which was continuing to jump from state to state. Arthur persisted with the aria ...

'Little will be left of me
In the coming by and by.'

Goddard was no longer listening. He was complimenting Raphael's painted backdrop. Arthur's song ended. He limped offstage to be replaced by a group of prancing dragoons. Goddard had seen enough. Oh for an evening of Don Giovanni. Holidays coming up. A few nights at Covent Garden would wash away the memory of ... this. 'Reduced with rouge indeed!'

'Not quite Wagner, is it Father?'

Brigadier Bryce-Jones, who was advising on the uniforms, had come downstairs from the chess tournament.

'You know I cannot abide Wagner, Brigadier. Far too repetitive. Besides, the whole concept of mortality of Deity may be theatrically promising, but spiritually I find it unsound.'

Bryce-Jones nodded politely and beat a hasty retreat.

'You'll put your head into the tournament upstairs before tea? We're on the last round now. Your team is in the final.'

'Of course!' replied Goddard, ambiguously. Then he crossed backstage into the dressing rooms. In the first, three of the dragoons were lounging before the mirrors. They rose and chorused, 'Afternoon Father.'

'Sit down, sit down. You look very convincing, I must admit.' He knew how to lie diplomatically when it suited. He had acquired the useful technique of admiring the scenery while tactfully ignoring the performance. Hardy, Sackville and Peterson were all members of the 'God Squad' and no matter how shoddy the production they had to sparkle.

'How does it feel to be a soldier of the Queen?' asked Goddard, taking a seat on the dressing-room bench—a move designed to encourage frankness. Sackville, a prefect and possibly the nearest favourite to Benjamin, answered first.

'Rather hot and uncomfortable, Father. Not as good as your production of "Journeys End".'

Peterson loosened his collar. 'Is this the sort of uniform they wore in the Crimea?'

'Pretty well. Intolerable during the day, but at night you'd be grateful for it.'

Lady Jane entered and flashed flirtatiously at the assembled petty officers. 'Hello boys.' There was no response. Moving further into the room, he saw Goddard.

'Hello Father,' he stammered. 'Did you like the aria?'

Goddard rose. 'Not bad, Arthur. I thought you would do better to mug at the audience less. There's no need to beg their appreciation.'

Arthur crossed into the other changing room, unbuttoned the dress, stepped out of it, and was revealed as a pale slender boy with dark curly hair in grotesque make-up, his left leg supported by an iron brace. He said, 'It's awfully difficult singing and pretending to play the cello. And the other thing is . . . d'you think I should sing it seriously?' He began wiping the make-up off his face—a rather complicated effort as he needed his glasses throughout the operation.

'I keep remembering it's a funny opera—you know, funny ha-ha, but actually, what Lady Jane's singing about is rather sad.' All make-up now removed, he began the long process of dressing from his underpants to complete senior suit for the evening meal. 'I feel, Father, I shouldn't take the mickey. Actually I'd rather do "Iolanthe"—do you know "Iolanthe"? —or even a more serious opera like those you told us . . .'

'He's gone, Arthur,' droned Hardy in deliberately moronic fashion. Now out of uniform, he hung round the door in his underwear and made a gesture with his hand to the effect that

Arthur never knew when to keep quiet. He then accompanied the silent word 'wanker' with the appropriate gesture.

Arthur shrugged it off and smiled in an awkward way. His whole manner was apologetic. This very anxiety to please only spurred his tormentors' delight.

'You got a good tan. I'm going to get one this holiday. We might be going to North Africa.'

Some voice shouted, 'Pack it in Janie. We've got a show tonight.'

'Yes, yes, got to be in good voice,' Arthur agreed.

Goddard was on his way to his study, via the windowed corridor which joined the teaching and dormitory wings. Here was a busy silence. All around clusters of boys in the small day rooms playing chess under Bryce-Jones. Goddard acknowledged him with a nod. A few heads turned, then returned in silence to the central match between Stanfield from Lacey House (Goddard's own) and Scott from Parson House (Brigadier Bryce-Jones' regiment). Goddard decided not to stay but offered a silent prayer for victory.

The afternoon was becoming quite sunny, though the spring chill remained. Goddard was midway between the stairwells at each end of the top corridor when he first saw the black and chrome figure through the window. The sound of the big Triumph shattered the afternoon as it roared past the front gate. The rider did not stop, but the very presence of that howling beast anywhere in the vicinity annoyed Goddard.

He resumed his journey towards his study and the remaining unmarked exam papers. Then he heard the machine change direction, gathering speed back up the road, back towards his realm. Its tyres crunched over the pebble path and went past the gatehouse without stopping. Goddard's feet doubled into a run. Down the stairs, stopping at the ground-floor door, waiting a moment before walking slowly into the covered archway beneath, facing the main drive.

The bike screeched to a standstill in a scattering of gravel. Goddard did not miss a beat, but continued at his floating pace until, framed by the honey-grey central arch, he stopped and turned towards the black figure in the centre of the drive as if he had only noticed him just at that precise moment. A falcon's eyes are flashing gems before the kill; their beauty dazzles the hunted.

Goddard ruled his little kingdom with that savage instinct, keeping his fine intelligence for the classroom and the kingdom of God. He noticed the black, brown and blond heads gathered at the windows to see the intruder.

The creature across the circle also noticed. He could see the curious faces and tossed his head in a sort of salute, like a garlanded bull. Dribbles of laughter greeted him from the arena. Goddard stiffened. The eyes widened, then narrowed to the challenge. He almost moved. In spite of himself his hands had almost clapped the voyeurs away from the windows. A tactical error. Most of them were unaware of his presence. Besides, this duel needed the third force—the audience. And so he waited in silence for the second challenge from the dark rider.

Blakey took off his helmet. A cascade of thick greasy curls fell from the visored crown to frame his face. He shook them away from his face and scratched his head. He placed the helmet on the seat of the bike between his legs, waving again at the crowd. Then he looked directly at Goddard. The victim had declared himself available. The Hound of God moved out from beneath the covered way. Several heads in the galleries above vanished at his entry on the scene. Most stayed to watch.

Goddard's eyes were on the bull, who was holding his ground. His pace quickened. 'Don't let him alight.' The victim came into focus. Tall, young, the hair—predictable, sun-blown face, old leather and filthy denim. Typical. Not quite so tall as at first imagined. A good deal older too. 'Now. Make him speak first with a slight inviting smile,' he thought.

'Hello Vicar.'

Don't bite yet, thought Goddard, eyes asparkle at the possibilities of the encounter.

'Yes, my son,' he replied, with consummate politeness.

'Anything doing?'

'I beg your pardon?'

'Got any work?' it explained.

No reply, for the moment, as the priest eyed the man and machine from head to wheel. There was a remarkable incongruity in the hands, which were large but beautifully proportioned. The nails were well kept ... of course—the guitar strapped across the back.

'Any odd jobs around the school. Head cook, bottle washer —you wi'me?'

A faint smell of Scotland in the grunts, thought Goddard, and returned to the face.

'We sometimes advertise in the town ten miles further down this road. There's no current vacancy so far as I'm aware.' Goddard shifted slightly, expecting the man to leave. Instead Blakey smiled and returned Goddard's stare with a wily ease.

'Are you the gaffer?' he asked. Goddard frowned, not from ignorance of the word but to signal that the conversation was at an end. Blakey pointed past the priest at the grass terraces across the courtyard. Goddard was about to speak when Blakey continued amiably, 'I could do you a nice rock garden over there, alpine flowers, waterfall, very artistic.'

Not turning to look at the terraces, Goddard stared fiercely at Blakey. His lip curled in a lethal silent 'Go'. He gestured towards the roadway.

'Ay right, I know when I'm not wanted, Padre.' Blakey placed the helmet back onto his head, lifting the visor to speak. 'And you brother can go forth and fuck yerself. Fuckin' crow.'

The bike started, reared on the drive, and then headed back towards the entrance. The rider made a familiar gesture towards the audience of boys concerning his respect for Goddard.

Goddard smiled. A defeat acknowledged. He clapped his hands at a group of giggling spectators from the junior school. They immediately disappeared. He then surveyed the front of Sommerbury. Not a face was visible. Perhaps a few lurkers in the shadows or behind the half closed window on the bridge passage. No, one face was completely visible.

Framed in the open window two floors above, as Goddard had been framed by the arch beneath, was Benjamin Stanfield. He smiled his half smile as Goddard walked smartly back into the covered way. Another voice turned Benji's head.

'Stanfield! What are you doing here, fellow? You're supposed to be playing a chess tournament, not staring out across the meadow. Come on fellow, move yourself!' This kind of command, even from that imperious old dullard, Bryce-Jones, only increased Benjamin's languor.

'I was just watching Father give that bikie fellow his marching orders ... sir.' The phrases were a deliberate mockery of Bryce-Jones, who referred to everyone as 'fellow'.

'Watching what, fellow? Go on inside and get on with the game. Scot has made his move.' Bryce-Jones stared out at the empty courtyard and saw nothing but the tyre marks on the pebble drive.

Benji caught a swift glance of the rider through another window, as he spoke to the gatekeeper, before disappearing from sight, the purr of the bike lingering across the fields.

'Benjamin! I shan't warn you again, fellow.'

It was plain from his tone that Benjamin was winning the match against Bryce-Jones' champion.

'If you aren't interested in the tournament, I'll have you raking the driveway to keep you occupied.'

Without a word Benjamin returned to the chess.

Bryce-Jones shouted out of the window at a group of boys gathering round the scene of the incident, 'You fellow. Yes, you know who I mean. Go and get a rake and make yourself useful. Clean up the drive. Now, fellow.'

The voice from below bleated some excuse about rehearsal and a performance that night.

'Well, delegate, fellow, but if that yard is not raked I'm holding you responsible.'

'But sir.'

'Move yourself, fellow!'

Early that evening, Benji sat opposite Goddard with a volume of Gerard Manly Hopkins on his knees. There was an hour to fill before the evening meal and the performance of 'Patience'. Goddard had summoned him to his study to compliment him on his essay and to introduce him to some of the poetry, in hopes of his reading it during the holiday. He returned the book to Goddard who, after an intake of breath, began to read aloud.

Benji watched him intently. He was mesmerised by the firmness and simplicity with which the voice enlivened the complexity of images. The boy sank deep into the leather armchair, ravished by the sounds of

> 'How to keep
> Back beauty, keep it, beauty,
> Beauty, beauty
> From vanishing away?'

He repeated the phrase, emphasising its question and looked up briefly at his listener, whose eyes had closed to hold the word pictures. And read on, referring to the text only occasionally, for he had taken it all to heart a long time ago—

> 'O is there no frowning of those wrinkles
> ranked wrinkles deep,
> Down? No waving off of these
> most mournful messengers,
> still messengers, sad and
> stealing messengers of grey . . .'

A shout from the dormitory nearby of 'Give me that back, Dyson, you spastic', and a bellow of 'Quiet!' failed to part the thread between voice and listener. Only slight irritation pinched Goddard's face, nothing more. His concentration dived again into the melodious pool of—

> 'No there's none, there's none,
> O no, there's none
> Nor can you long be, what you
> are now, called fair . . .'

Goddard pointed the lines directly at Benji, who had opened his eyes. He smiled. Goddard read on.

> 'Do what you may do, what, do
> what you may
> And wisdom is early to despair:
> Be beginning
> Be beginning to despair
> O there is none; no, no, no,
> there's none:
> Be beginning to despair, to despair,
> Despair, despair, despair, despair.'

23

Benji had stopped listening at the first despair, watching the priest chime the word in, in, in, into himself, the earlier sensuality of the language warping to a toneless rasp: despair, despair. Silence.

'So,' said Goddard, glaring at an unseen disturbance again from the dormitory, 'the poem may seem difficult in places . . .'

'You say it well, Father,' interrupted Benji.

'Thank you, yes . . . It is a wonderful poem and must be served well. The subject of the poem is clear enough. It's about—'

'Beauty,' said Benjamin immediately. Goddard nodded. 'Physical beauty,' Benji added.

'Physical beauty exactly.' Goddard rose and ambled round the room to a point between the door and Benji's armchair. 'Beauty,' he murmured, 'physical beauty. Why despair?'

'Because . . .' (Benji's head arched around but could not see the speaker without rising from the chair)

'Go on,' urged the voice. 'Why despair?'

Benji turned to look again towards the small fire bristling in the grate. 'Because beauty's been given to us only to be taken away again,' he said.

Goddard swung round the room to face him. 'Good boy. In this first poem, "The Leaden Echo", Hopkins shows that what seems our finest possession, our beauty, youthful vigour, is that which is taken from us in the most terrible way. What then is the answer to this? What does "The Golden Echo" say?'

Benjamin did not answer immediately though he knew exactly what he was going to say. When he knew a response perfectly he always affected his softer voice; it was a studied device that Goddard found irresistible. For when he spoke thus, that slight sibilance, that imperfect 'r' sound, emanating from his sturdy frame made the boy seem deceptively vulnerable.

'That we should give beauty back to God. It is from him that beauty comes.'

Goddard's sentiment spilled into Benjamin's answer. 'Yes, yes! Here, where it is most precious to us . . . while it is still ours to give. In heaven, beauty has an everlasting quality.'

Benji nodded his understanding. Goddard took the book

again and began to read 'The Golden Echo'.

> 'Yes, I can tell such a key
> I do know such a place
> Where what was prized and
> passes of us ...'

Benjamin Stanfield was not the most beautiful boy in the form. Nor was physical beauty a criterion for advancement. Sackville, or even Hardy, were by classical standards beautiful. In fact, in the boarding-school setting, Sackville, with his blond hair and statuesque build, was the pretty one. Goddard found him leaden and slow. Benjamin, on the other hand, was quick as fire, and as bright. There was a burning energy, an intensity to know about things. His personality was a curious blend of charm and emotional distance. It was this that many of his adult admirers found attractive, taking it for a sort of maturity, though a combustible mixture lay beneath.

Benji's father was wealthy and a drunk. He sent useless expensive presents at birthdays and Christmas. His mother had remarried when he was very young. She was already carrying his stepbrother before the separation. Most of Benji's life had been spent at Sommerbury; the various teacher priests had been mother and father to him.

But above all it was his eminence, Father Goddard, who fired his imagination and silently adored his triumphs on the playing field. The priest had no illusions about the boy. His ambiguous, competitive personality needed careful handling. At its worst it was deeply malicious. Witness to that came from Father Gladstone.

Benjamin infuriated the sports master by his disregard for planned playing tactics and his arrogant disrespect for team effort. Benjamin was a soloist who followed his intuition to score try after try. On the rare occasions when he was outsmarted by an opponent, he would lose his temper on the field but wait several matches to take his revenge on the marked player. This young god in the newness of his power was lethal when challenged—something he had learnt from Father Goddard.

But he carried his success well and lorded over the other boys with grace, accepting their favoured respect and admiration. And just as Goddard was deputy while Father Rivers was the titular head, so Benjamin was deputy school captain to Sackville's Head Boy. As above, so below. 'Fame cannot better be held nor more attained than by a place below the first.' Shakespeare might have learned that from a Jesuit, for their power is concentrated in that vital hold, just below the first, where great freedom of movement is unhampered by responsibility or exposure.

> '... everything that's
> fresh and fast flying of us,
> seems so sweet, of us and
> swiftly away with, done with
> soon done with, and yet dearly
> and dangerously sweet ...'

With Goddard it was a matter of chemistry—his special caring for a boy like Stanfield. He was well aware of the problem that was not a problem but nevertheless is, world without end in the world without women, amen.

> 'The Flower of Beauty, fleece of
> beauty too, too apt to ah!
> to fleet ...'

He had passed through that treacherous labyrinth, unscathed by even the slightest flirtation, unsullied by even the merest momentary lapse. No form of adultery had outraged the sacred marriage he had with Christ. His soul was bridal white. He was proud that he had loved no one but the One. Though in his capacity as a Master and a Priest he had to deal with such relationships, he always used discretion (and, when it suited him, a small dose of compassion), but never wavered from his interpretation of the teachings of the Church. Love of that kind was not love but an abomination. Boys and younger priests he had to instruct on the matter would be reminded that each moment in the state of gracelessness was another wound on the crucified body of Christ—Christ, the Lover of lovers, whose embrace was eternal.

26

'Never fleets more, fastened with
the tenderest truth
To its own best being and its
loveliness of youth : it is an
everlastingness of,
O it is all youth.'

The man and the youth sat facing each other, in silence, in stillness. A log in the small fire burnt through, disintegrating into the cold ashes below. Benjamin nodded at Goddard with that enigmatic half smile. Goddard handed him the open book.

'Would you put it back on the shelf for me Benji, please.' A knock on the door. 'Yes. Enter.' Gale and Reiner tumbled in, followed a length behind by Arthur Dyson.

'Father ...'

'Yes Gale, what is it?' The intrusion was not welcome but inevitable at this time of day.

'Could we watch the football on TV now ...'

'Not tonight.'

'Oh Father, it's an international!' said Gale.

'Direct from Rome,' added Arthur, hoping a mention of the Holy City might change his mind.

'I wouldn't care if the Vatican were playing Canterbury twelve-a-side.'

'But Father ...' the boys groaned.

'That's enough, Dyson. Take that whine out of your voice. I said no and I mean no. Besides, it's nearly dinner and then there is "Patience". You must start to learn to make choices. There's not enough time for everything.'

Gale spoke first. 'Yes Father. Thank you.'

Rainer and Arthur were looking across the room at Benji, who had put the book on a table and was quietly abstracting the large ornate African spear from the umbrella stand by the bookcase. As they left, Arthur gave Benji an encouraging smile. Benji ignored it. The game was not for that creep's benefit but for himself alone. Goddard turned and saw him holding the spear aloft, a young Masai, armoured only in sunlight and white plumes, advancing across the study towards him with a weird aggressive smile, the tip of the blade lowering in towards the master's sacred heart.

Benji tested the game. Blandly he asked, 'From West Africa, Father?'

Gently Goddard replied, 'That's right. Put it back now.' But the spear still pointed at the priest's heart. Goddard took a book from the table at his side—by chance, his breviary. He held it aloft in his left hand, like every holy picture of St Francis Xavier with Benji as the pagan warrior. He placed the book of his divine office against his heart. The tip of the blade touched the black leather cover.

'Back where it belongs, boy,' warned Goddard.

Outside the small room, bells in the school rang the hungry faithful to the evening meal.

Blakey wheeled the big Triumph into the twilight of Basket Wood. Leaving the bike, he scouted north a couple of hundred yards to the edge of the clearing; he was on the school estate. It was a safe and comfortable camping ground for an evening —maybe a few days if he was lucky. The wooded rise shrouded the clearing from the school, the trees along the river bank hid it from the road— The chosen patch of ground was dominated by two trees—the smaller, fallen and dying, the other, standing majestically on a part of the ridge, very much alive. Its root system had been completely exposed by flooding but it never-theless stood safe, its great tendrils clutching out over the whole area. Here was an ideal sanctuary to make camp; the bike could be concealed in the enormous hollow beneath the roots. A man could stand or lie there with ease, almost dis-appearing from view into the tabernacle beneath the trunk. In the faint evening light the clearing resembled an arboreal cathedral: branches for vaulting ribs, the fallen tree an altar, a coverlet of brambles and thorns, the dank root-chamber a pagan confessional or a holy of holies.

The bells from the school sounded across the woodland nave. The erl-king may have a great castle to spend the night in but the larder is bare. Plenty of fish in the river but after travelling all day it would be too much work in the fast fading light to catch anything.

'More bells ... that black bastard crow and his little blue-blazered buggers are stuffing themselves over there. I think

28

I'll help myself to their charity,' he thought.

He took off his visored helm and strapped it to his charger. Expertly he unpacked and set about arranging his throne-room and bed-chamber. A few years in the navy had made him scrupulously well-organised—even down to the dry kindling rolled into his sleeping bag. He would start a small fire on his return from the raiding party on the other kingdom. He finished unpacking and stowed the guitar away among the roots now covered with a silver-grey tarpaulin. He rolled a smoke and sauntered up the ridge till he could see the school ablaze with lights half a mile across the velvet night fields. He paused at the rim to finish his smoke. Nice dope ... scored last night in Birmingham. Dealing himself from time to time, he knew the right people and the right places. Dragging on the sweet weed, squatting on his haunches, the Woodland King was transformed into a malevolent gargoyle, broad black leather shoulders, red stubble chin pressed onto greasy denim knees, white face, a wild demonic grin, singing a war song softly to himself.

'When the moon is black, billy boy, my lad
We'll take to the fields and the river
And up to the hold of the laird we'll go
On tippy toe, on tippy tippy toe
And rob him blind of his venison and wine
And steal a kiss of his lady love
From right beneath his very nose, billy boy,
From beneath his bloody nose.'

Well Blakey boy, my lad, the moon is black tonight. He slipped from sight into the fields, into the kingdom of Goddard for the second time.

The evening meal over, the family of St Anthony's had moved into the ballroom for the first and last performance of 'Patience'. Though a private affair for staff, students and household, it was graced by the presence of Father Rivers who was, fortunately, well enough to attend. As he entered he was met by a pre-ordained but nonetheless rousing cheer from the school.

Mrs Hoskins, who supervised the domestic staff, took pride

of place on these occasions and sat in the centre stalls with Father Rivers. Her contribution to the evening would come after the curtain fell when the official party and final year contingent retired to the masters' rooms for the buffet supper she and her staff had spent all day preparing. She had travelled to the village for an elaborate perm which sat on her head like spun candy but gave off the odour of varnish shampoo. Father Goddard sat on the right hand of Father Rivers.

Father Henry entered with his baton, made a special nod to Father Rivers and tapped the music stand. There was a burst of applause. Rather than starting, he waved the orchestra to stand and acknowledge the applause. Finally they sat and the play began. The orchestra managed to make sense of some of the tunes in the overture. On the whole though, it remained an incoherent battery of barps and farts.

Goddard rolled his eyes to heaven, steeling himself for an evening of unrelieved ineptitude. He beckoned to a prefect and told him to instruct Stanfield and Gale to keep the groundlings under strict supervision. If the prophecy of the overture was fulfilled there would be many unscheduled laughs.

Benjamin decided to supervise the group nearest the door to allow himself a break for a cigarette. He could also encourage catcalls when Arthur minced on as Lady Jane. The orchestra revved up to a series of catatonic thumps heralding the curtain's rise as the house lights fell to half before the faulty lighting board plunged the entire auditorium into darkness. Through the stygian gloom, Father Henry hissed instructions at the incompetent responsible.

The orchestra lights were plugged back in, revealing a giggling second violin sticking his bow into the ear of the trombone behind.

'David, behave!' hissed Father Henry. 'All right everyone, pick it up from letter "B".'

Goddard stood to face the noisiest section of the stalls. 'That's enough, gentlemen.' Giggles stifled into silence.

The one spot operator, suddenly given light, anticipated his cue, flooding Father Goddard with a blaze of Lady Jane's straw and pink. Goddard turned to the stage where the curtain flew away to reveal twenty lovesick maidens. He sat, murmuring, 'For what we are about to receive, Lord have mercy.'

A half-open basement window gave the intruder easy access to the school buildings. Blakey dragged himself astride the ledge and then paused to acknowledge a burst of applause from the adjacent building. The corridor beneath him was in darkness, so he dropped his haversack to the floor to judge the distance his probing foot could not fathom. It was three times the drop to the ground outside. He eased himself over until he was hanging by his fingertips, then slid to the floor. He looked back up. Getting out may be a problem, he thought. His stomach rumbled, dismissing the problem from his mind.

Softly he felt his way along to a stairwell, then up to a wooden door. Across another passage was a door with an inset glass panel—the kitchen. Padlocked. 'Shit a brick, vicar,' he murmured, 'you're not making things easy for the starving and homeless.' From his boot he drew a knife and set about the lock: After a few minutes of frustration, expertise gave way to expediency and brute force opened it. It fell to the floor with a leaden clang. He examined the knife. Broken—the tip wedged into the lock. He threw it angrily across the hall.

Inside the kitchen rows of savouries and sandwiches were laid out ready for the supper after the performance. With his big hands he picked up the daintiest of fish-paste squares and placed it delicately on his tongue. With his little finger he mimed genteelly wiping the corners of his mouth. A further fistful of delicacies he swallowed without ceremony, washing it down with a glass of cheap red wine before setting about filling the haversack with as much as he could from the tables, benches and shelves. The singing, seeming momentarily louder, caught his attention again.

'Now isn't this ridiculous
And isn't this preposterous
A thorough-paced absurdity
Explain it if you can . . .'

A large honeyroast ham caught his eye. Quickly he emptied tins and bottles from the haversack to make room for this prize. The business of the evening being complete, he decided a toast to his gracious but unwitting hosts was in order. 'The toast is the black buzzards of Rome!' he cried softly. He raised a glass and threw the contents down his throat, wine

31

running out of the corners of his mouth and over his neck. 'Not bad ... a very good month, don't you know.' Again he raised the glass in mocking salute. In quick succession he downed another, then another ... 'just one more for luck' ... till he had drunk about ten glassfuls in all. The drink and the dope were beginning to have an effect. He washed his hands in the punch, then blessed himself with it. 'I'll leave that for the service tomorrow,' he chuckled. A wrapped bottle caught his eye. 'What have we here ... ?' He opened the gift and discovered a bottle of black label whisky intended for Father Henry. 'You shouldn't have. God, you're good to me.' After checking that the top was screwed on tight he jammed this final valuable into the bulging swag.

Once outside the kitchen, he bent to pick up the knife nearby and shoved it into the bag. The wine hit him hard. He hiccuped violently and fell to his knees. He got up, belched and shuddered. 'Down boy ... down, down ... Shit! Which way out?'

Back at his starting point, he found it impossible to reach the high window by which he had entered. Awkwardly he retraced his steps, up to the kitchen corridor, past the open door and the desecration within, finally reaching a long windowed hallway adjacent to the dining hall. Through the windows he could see the courtyard, the terraces and the fields, but no way out and no lights. A sound. Someone was coming down the hallway. He began to panic. A glass door closed. He froze. The black soutaned figure drifted slowly out of the darkness towards him. No place to hide.

Contact. The bent figure of Father Pollard was directly before him, the old priest fingering his rosary beads and murmuring prayers to himself.

'Good evening. God bless you,' came the automatic greeting. 'God bless you,' mumbled Blakey as the old man drifted out of sight. 'God bless you indeed.'

Further along the corridor he found an open door. With great relief he stepped out into the courtyard and the open air. It hit him in the face, almost knocking him off-balance.

'The moon is black tonight ...' he sang to himself. 'Bugger that wine.' Abruptly he pulled back into the shadow of the doorway. 'What's that?'

Benji hid the lighted cigarette in his cupped hand. Whoever

it was was standing directly in his path to the kitchen. Father Moore had asked him to start preparing the table—a chance for a cigarette and a few sips of wine. The shadow in the doorway didn't move. Benji slowed his pace. A thought occurred—one of the boys is raiding the kitchen. He enjoyed the idea of discovering someone in a compromising position: it would give him an opportunity to try out his repertoire of Goddardisms. But how had the boy got in? Unless he broke the lock. There was only one key and Benji had that.

The shadow in the doorway was someone else. In his excitement he conjured a formidable adversary. Across the yard there was a sudden movement. Benji dragged nervously on the cigarette, his hand shaking, the orange glow bobbing in the dark like a demented firefly.

Blakey smelt the fear and took his chance. He broke cover, leaped at the boy, and screamed at him like a wildman. 'It's Him ... Him ... Him from this afternoon!' The drunken figure staggered into a run and after him ran Benji.

Wine and the unfamiliar terrain slowed the flier. He stumbled across the flowerbeds and tripped down the terraces in his desperation to find the way back to the wood. Benji, the champion athlete, found it easy to close the distance between them. When they reached the flatness of the playing fields he was less than ten yards from his quarry. Midfield—between the two kingdoms—Blakey stopped, caught his breath, and turned to face his pursuer. He dumped the loot, reaching instinctively for the knife in his boot. It was then that Benji hit him in a blind flying tackle. Knees, fists and elbows reduced the intruder to a grunting heap on the moist dark grass. The dance began. Blakey, the enraged animal desperate to survive the hunter's first assault, quickly recovered. He pitched the boy over him, then leapt astride to pin him flat on his back, gripping his body between his thighs, grasping his wrists in his strong hands. But Benji was lithe and powerful, and twisted one arm free, to take a wild swing at Blakey's face.

'Jimmy, Jimmy, I'm not going to hurt you. Easy now, okay?' Benji recovered enough breath to howl, 'Father! Father! ...' Blakey jammed his mouth over Benji's, squeezing his chest hard between his knees. Shock more than pain stifled the sound. 'Father! Fa...Fa...'

In wild eyed silence, Benji stared at the monster that had

33

sucked out his voice. It was as though in one strange violent kiss, Blakey had drawn the sound into his belly, sucked the air out of him, swallowed the name with it, and left him empty. The enchanter spoke, softly.

'All right. Enough.' He released his hold. Benji responded with terrifying vehemence, raking and gouging with his nails any flesh he could find. 'Give in,' he yelled, with as much authority as he could muster.

'You're jokin'.' Blakey began to laugh.

'It's my fight, you fucking gyppo.'

Blakey laughed again and pinioned Benji once more. 'All right, we're even then,' Benji conceded, pain watering into his eyes. 'Let go.'

'No, you let go.'

'Count to three and both let go together.'

'Schoolboy games, is it?'

Both of them counted, Blakey between laughs. Warily they disentangled and crept apart to survey their individual damage. Blakey spat onto the grass. He found some blood on his finger. It wasn't his.

'I think you must be bleeding somewhere.'

'Mouth,' said Benji. Blakey reached across to his foe and cursorily examined the face.

'You'll live. Another one up there,' said Blakey, gently pushing the hair out of the boy's eyes. Benji recoiled instinctively from the touch. 'Does it hurt?'

'No.'

Blakey took the whisky from his bag, unwrapped it and poured some down his throat. He offered the bottle to Benji. He refused.

'Come on, laddie, seal your victory with a swill of the old fire-water.' Benji took the bottle and wet his lips, but didn't swallow. The whisky stung into the cut and he spat it out. Blakey laughed and tousled Benji's hair. 'Get it down ya.' Benji drank, aping Blakey's bravura style, guzzling it violently. 'You're pretty strong, lad . . . for a pouffy schoolgirl. Mind you, you've got God on your side.' Benji smiled to himself in the darkness. He knew who he called 'God'. Blakey took the bottle back.

Rousing applause came from the school. The lights in the courtyard came full on. Boys began to spill out of the hall.

Blakey gathered his belongings together. 'Listen, laddie, don't sell my hide to the crows.' He disappeared into the night. Benjamin saw his silhouette on the clearing's edge. Then the wood covered him completely with night.

Benji ran back to the school, doubling completely round the building to make his entrance across the drive and through the archway at the front. Father Moore had discovered the pillage and was stalking angrily across the courtyard when Benji ran up to him.

'Father, Father, I just chased ... chased ... he's stolen our food, and ...' Benji exaggerated the breathlessness.

'Benjamin, are you hurt?'

'Yes Father but ... he's run away down to his ... he's gone towards the village ...'

'Did this fellow hit you?'

'No Father ... I was running so fast ... I fell ... but our supper is ruined ...'

'Now don't you worry about that. Quickly, upstairs and clean up. I'll ask Father Goddard to keep people in the hall, while we get some order into the kitchen.'

'What's happened to Benji?' asked Sackville, joining them in the kitchen.

'Never you mind. Tell Mrs Hoskins what's happened. Get a few fellows from Lacey House to help Cook. I'll speak to Father Goddard. Benjamin, go upstairs and wash those cuts.'

Benjamin, filled with the night's excitement, undressed with fumbling fingers. As he took off his trousers his legs gave under him and he fell to the floor. He sat a while, laughing at his over-excitement. Once in the shower, he recalled the whole extraordinary sequence of events. His imagination reran the chase, refought the duel. He flooded the encounter with mystic significance in wild kingdoms beyond the realms of God. In that fight, Benjamin had crossed a threshold of experience; in that breathless, bloody encounter with that powerful other body he had sensed the limits of his own strength. He had met an opposite and equal force. He wanted more of it. The exultant victory on the track, the powerful drive down the wing to score could not match the power of that night.

He examined his body in the shower—the cuts on his face were minor. His knees and shins were bruised red, and there was a red throbbing mark on his chest. His hands were scorched green by the grass and his wrists still bore the white incisions of Blakey's nails. The water poured over him. He loved his wounds, and the soapy inspection became a caress. He realized he was sexually aroused. In embarrassment he turned to hide himself, concentrating on splashing water onto his hair and face. He swallowed large gulps to wash out his injured mouth, reliving the terror of his vulnerability when the barbarian tore out his voice and swallowed it. He shuddered.

As he stepped from the shower and began carefully to dry himself, Goddard's voice echoed across the gleaming marble. 'Benjamin.'

'Yes Father. Come in.' Goddard walked into the room. Benjamin covered his nakedness with a towel.

'Are you all right?'

'Yes Father. I ran after the man who broke into the kitchen.'

'Yes, Father Moore has told me. I've brought you some antiseptic cream for the cuts. Show me.'

'Here ... and here ...'

'Not too bad.' Goddard dried them with cotton wool and expertly dabbed the ointment into the small cuts, anointing the boy's mouth and forehead. 'You're quite bruised. Did you make contact with him?'

'No Father, I just fell over into the ditch.'

'Did you see what he looked like?'

'No Father, it was all happening so quickly. I just ran after him. He laughed. The faster I ran, the faster he ran. In the panic I fell into a ditch. The worst bruise is here on my chest —see ...' He proffered his chest to Goddard to touch.

'Yes, yes, I can see. Don't get cold.'

Benjamin had never noticed before how Goddard tensed at any physical contact, nor how his nakedness unnerved him. Goddard turned to go, and was met at the door by a group of boys.

'What are you doing here? You should be at the reception. Sackville, I'm surprised at you. Return to the reception room immediately. Arthur. Why are you here boy?'

'I was just wanting to see Benji, Father ...'

'It's none of your business, Dyson. Besides after your performance tonight I'm surprised you can drag yourself away

36

from the party. Come on, leave Benjamin to dress.'

'You'll tell us about it later eh, Benji?' cried Arthur as he disappeared out of the showers. Benji ignored him.

On his way back to the reception, Goddard changed direction to his study, where he took a brown scapula from his drawer.

Benjamin was in the enclosed dormitory cubicle that served as his bedroom, standing with his towel round his waist examining his wounds in the mirror. He looked up nervously as Father Goddard called him. 'Benjamin. I was concerned when I heard you were hurt. I would like you to wear this.'

He held out the scapula. Benjamin stepped forward, but instead of taking it from him, bowed his head as though to accept a decoration. Goddard widened the cord with his fingers and placed it over the boy's head.

'Wear Our Lady near your heart. She will protect you.'

'Thank you Father.'

'. . . and keep you safe, Benji.' The priest removed his hand from the cloth medallion and let it drop onto the boy's chest. Benji looked down at it. He adjusted it to the centre of his chest so as not to obscure the victorious blast of red that was swelling on his left pectoral. At that moment, Goddard sprang his urgent question.

'Was the thief the man on the bike who was sent packing this afternoon?'

Benjamin answered no. He took his towel off and stood naked before the priest. Goddard turned away, stepped out of the bedroom and pulled the curtain. Benji smiled as he pulled on his pyjama pants. He had never lied to Goddard's face before. Another threshold had been crossed. He sensed again how uncomfortable his nakedness made Goddard. It had helped him lie. But more than that, it had exposed 'God'. In that moment he had smelt Goddard's fear—the newest, sweetest smell he had ever breathed.

Fifteen minutes before lights out is the least regimented time of the boys' day. The atmosphere is generally subdued. Most of the talk, much to Arthur's chagrin, was not about the play but about Benjamin's performance. The mystery was deepened by Benjamin's determined seclusion in his cubicle where he sat alone, revelling in the notoriety but secure in the secrecy of his encounter. Beneath the buzz of the dying day Gale and Rainer sat on their beds improvising twelve-bar blues on their guitars. Benjamin enjoyed the music. He remembered that on first sighting, the future raider had, that afternoon, carried a guitar.

Hanley was reading yet another James Michener novel, the first hundred pages had already taken a term. Hardy was writing a letter to his girlfriend at St Catherine's, their sister school in the next county. Arthur clumped in from the wash-room. He made the mistake of interrupting Hardy just as he was writing that the production would have been better if it had been a co-operative effort between the schools and his girlfriend had essayed Lady Jane. 'You were great tonight, Dominic.' Hardy ignored the compliment. Arthur moved away from him and turned his attention to Cawley and Manning who were playing chess in the cubicle opposite.

'You're in my light, Arthur,' grunted Manning, without looking up. 'Move yourself.' Manning picked up a piece, tapped it a couple of times on the board, then placed it down. Arthur felt he should correct an obvious mistake.

'Oh no, Mannie . . .'

'What's wrong?' said Manning.

Cawley, who stood to profit by Manning's tactical error, glared at the bespectacled interloper. 'Arthur, you're dripping all over my pawns.'

'Oh. Sorry, Michael.' He patted Cawley's arm, 'but Mannie should move rook to bishop six . . .'

Manning, frustrated by Arthur's interruptions, placed the pawn firmly where he had intended, ignoring Arthur's earnest suggestions. 'Do something useful. Jump out of a window.'

Arthur smiled his apologetic smile, oblivious to the insult as always. Cawley took Manning's queen.

'It's my game from here on.'

'There, you see,' lectured Arthur, 'see what I mean. Your move was dangerous, queen exposed, then she's gone.'

Manning accepted defeat with little grace. 'Fuck off Arthur. You distracted me.'

'I was only trying to help.'

Sackville walked across to Arthur and rescued him from Manning's wrath. 'Don't take it out on Arthur, Manning. You lost without his help.' Sackville had no special care for Arthur;

it was simply his responsibility to monitor the quiet time before bed.

Arthur's attention fell to Dowd, who was reading a letter from his latest Spanish conquest. What Spanish there was in the letter had been expertly translated by Raphael, who spoke the holiday language perfectly. A small audience had gathered in Dowd's cubicle for the reading. He handed the letter to Arthur.

'You read it, Arthur. She's got a very sexy voice—low. She's older than me of course, more mature . . . experienced and . . . you know.' Arthur smiled knowingly.

He began to read the letter in a low husky voice with what he believed to be a sexy accent. 'I will ever and only always be yours . . .' A few whistles from the crowd attested to the success of Arthur's interpretation. Dowd lay back on the bed.

'There's nothing better than a Spanish letter—except a French letter.'

This was met with a full-throated roar of appreciative laughter. Arthur, not wishing to lose his audience, read on. The Spanish accent getting somewhat lost in the process. As the text became more provocative, so its rendering moved northward to naughty post-card French.

'I cont ze daze till summer when I shall come in England and in your arms . . .' This sentence evoked genuine murmurs of appreciation from the gathering, '. . . until our lips meet and our languages touch . . .'

'What? Your what touches?' interrupted Gregory.

'Well, that's what it says,' said Arthur, proffering the letter.

'No, no, you stupid prick. Linguas—tongues touch,' insisted Raphael.

'Of course,' blushed Arthur, 'I should have known. I just got carried away.'

Benjamin left his bed and stood opposite the cubicle of international lovers. 'Fancy touching your scabby tongue, Dowd.' Dowd, already jerked from the warm embrace of his adolescent Lady of Spain, sat up. He loathed Stanfield.

'You can talk, Stanfield, you're the one that spends all day licking God's arse.'

Sackville cut in to end a situation that could have got out of hand, but to everyone's surprise, Benjamin did not flinch at the insult. Instead, he walked past Dowd towards Goddard's room. Dowd's voice followed him. 'Bet you made up all that rubbish about the thief, Stanfield, just like you to pull a stunt like that.'

'It wasn't a lark,' cried Arthur, 'it was for real. Benji was hurt.'

'You'll keep, Dowd,' called Benji.

'Any day, boy, any day,' answered Dowd.

'Wanker,' sneered Benji, leaving the dorm.

'Benji didn't make it up,' pleaded Arthur.

'Wouldn't put it past him,' sneered Dowd.

'You can talk,' interrupted Manning, still smarting from his chess defeat. 'This Spanish bit . . . what about her?'

'She's true. I lost my virginity to her.' There was a hush. Virginity and the rituals of adolescent sexuality were serious subjects. Voices lowered to a sanctuary reverence. 'She's really good at French kissing.'

'That's a mortal sin unless you're married.'

'Rubbish.'

'We are getting married. In three years, when she's eighteen.'

'Watch out you don't put her up the spout.'

'No. I'm careful.'

'Goddard'll see you roasting in the fires of eternal damnation if you got her pregnant and then pissed off.'

'Come off it, Arthur.'

The anonymity of the exchange was broken by Arthur's persistence about marriage. He continued, 'Father Goddard says that marriage is a much abused sacrament.'

'What does Goddard know about any of this, he's never had it,' said Dowd.

'And what about him and Stanfield?' said Dowd enthusiastically.

Arthur shifted his weight from one leg to the other, leaned into the group and began to perform his rarest and most treasured voice.

'Now Benji,' he intoned, invoking Goddard's presence with remarkable verisimilitude, 'our text for tonight is, "And the Lord said unto him, rise and come." '

A roar of laughter and thunderous applause brought Sackville down like an avenging angel. 'That's it. Lights out. Break it up.' Roughly he drew Arthur aside. 'You really make me

40

sick sometimes, Arthur, you're a little creep.'

'Sorry, Rupert, I was only making a joke. I don't really think that God and Benji are like that. We were only playing.'

Sackville pushed Arthur into his cubicle. 'All right, Arthur, just shut up and go to bed. If you could see yourself, sucking up to Dowd and Manning and them. Wake up to yourself. They don't give a shit about you. Just a warning, Arthur. If you keep on making up stories about Benjamin and Goddard I'll have to report you.'

'It wasn't me. It was Dowd's idea. He was the one that said it first.'

'Get ready for bed. I'm sick of the sight of you.'

'Rupert, you won't tell him, will you?'

'No, Arthur, but don't carry on, that's all.'

'You won't tell Benji either? Please. I really want to be friends with him.'

Sackville didn't answer, but shrugged away the pleading boy.

'Lights out everyone.'

'Good night. God bless.'

'Good night, God bless, Rupert,' sniffed Arthur.

'Night Arthur.'

Benji came out of Goddard's room. 'Benji,' gasped Arthur, 'Benji...'

'What is it?' Benjamin answered, without looking at him.

'I...er...I...you were really brave to chase him...the thief...I would have been scared to death. I don't think I could have done what you did.'

'No, Arthur, you couldn't. You've got a lump of metal on your leg and can't run.' It was said without malice and without kindness either.

'Of course. But I didn't mean it that way. I meant that—'

Benjamin drew his curtain. Goddard appeared in the doorway. He was dressed in long black trousers and a shabby grey sweater, his hands thrust low into his pockets.

'Come on, Dyson, you should be in bed. The play is over, the audience is asleep. So draw the curtain, Dyson.'

Arthur obeyed, joining the hidden chorus. 'Good night Father. God bless you.'

'Good night. God bless you all.'

The priest returned to marking the tests, finally falling into bed at two o'clock, resolving to use the first period after breakfast to discuss the Latin paper.

It was still dark when Benji crept out of his bed. Barefoot he walked across the cold shining corridors, up to the prefects' room at the top of the old house. From here, there was a superb view of the fields and the woods beyond. Out there, in the night, he thought he heard a distant guitar.

The cold of early morning froze him. He covered one foot with another, alternating them in a strange little dance as he strove to keep warm. His bare torso bubbled into goose-pimples, his nipples itched with the morning chill. The bruise on his chest was beginning to hurt when he breathed. He was on the point of returning to his bed when he saw a billow of ash and sparks from a fire deep in the wood flitter and hang in the quiet air like so many morning stars. So the greasy-haired Lucifer was awake and still in the woods. The dark morning lightened towards dawn. He turned away from the window and scampered down from the tower, back to his bed. Already his eagle hawk imagination was diving into the wood to seize the enchanter by the throat.

Part Two

MORNING'S MINION

Breakfast for the priest and the boys who served the morning mass always took place in a private room adjacent to the sacristy. While the rest of the school scrambled about the dining hall for their first meal of the day, this group would sit quietly discussing some theological topic chosen by the presiding priest. After ceremoniously removing their vestments, the priest and the head altar-boy would proceed to the table where the other servers waited.

Father Goddard and Benji entered the bright room. Mrs Hoskins, who had personally brought the breakfast across from the kitchen, was unusually sharp with Mary, one of the maids. She was muttering and scowling about the sacrilege committed upon her kitchen the night before. Father Goddard reassured her that the culprit would be caught and punished. He brought her wearisome banter to an abrupt close by making the sign of the cross. Benjamin said grace and the breakfast began.

Mrs Hoskins brought the steaming lumpy porridge to the side of the table leaving 'fat Mary' from the village to try to get it into the bowls. Goddard looked at the mud-grey ooze and decided to settle for orange juice alone.

'Thank God it's sunny today. Summer seems to have arrived at last.' This was Mrs Hoskins' cue to pack away the rolled oats and serve cornflakes at breakfast in future.

'Mary, serve Father's sausages and eggs now,' said Mrs Hoskins, 'I've got to get back to the kitchen.' Gale helped clear away the porridge bowls and lay the plates for the main course. Mary lumped across the room to slide the hot plate before the priest.

Mary leaned over Dominic Hardy, 'I thought you were very handsome in the play last night, Dom.'

43

'Thank you Mary,' replied Dominic. His handsomeness was rewarded with an extra sausage.

'You were very funny too, Arthur.' She awarded the comic Lady Jane the same grilled accolade.

'It wasn't supposed to be funny, Mary,' said Arthur bleakly.

'Mary,' said Benjamin, 'Could I have an extra sausage?'

'No you can't,' rasped the overweight girl, 'you're just being greedy, Benjamin Stanfield.' (Mary remembered well the afternoon when Benjamin had crept into the kitchen and jolted her ample bottom with a battery operated cow-prod.)

'You can have mine Benji,' said Arthur, proffering the sausage. Benjamin nodded his thanks and accepted the rather burnt offering. 'Take some tomato as well—I don't like grilled tomato.' Benjamin took most of what was on Arthur's plate, leaving a rather small piece of egg and a crusty half-eaten sausage.

'Leave me something,' whined Arthur.

'Well, you offered, Dyson.'

'Thank you, Mary,' said Goddard, 'we'll look after the tea and toast ourselves.'

'Thank you, Father, God bless you.' Mary left the room.

'Terence,' said Goddard to Cawley, 'when I give a gentle tap to the cruet with the chalice kindly stop pouring the wine.'

'Yes Father,' he responded, blushing that he should have been the first to be chosen to atone for his errors at Mass. 'Sorry, I wasn't paying attention.'

'Anyone would think you were trying to get me drunk.'

The boys laughed, more in surprise at the priest's good humour than at the joke. 'Last time we broke bread together after Mass we concluded our discussion on the sacrament of marriage. Today I want to talk about another sacrament, the sacrament of confession. Finish eating Gale, you can't possibly hear properly with your mouth full. Confession. Well, all of you have experienced the sacrament but it is important that you have a firm understanding of its nature. I once said that God is always looking for ways to show his love for us more deeply. This sacrament is a real way of doing just that. Confession is the means God has appointed for reconciling to himself members of His community who have strayed into serious sin. Sins are revealed to the priest only and in secret. Let's think about that for a moment.'

In the silence Goddard got up and began serving the tea to the boys. When he had filled the cups he returned to his place and sat down again. The boys administered various amounts of milk and sugar to the cups with reverent ceremony to sustain the serious mood of the discussion and offered toast and marmalade around the table. From now on, the discussion could continue between mouthfuls but the topic could not be changed.

'I also talked about absolution,' continued Goddard. 'What is absolution?'

'You said it was the means God uses to forgive our sins,' said Sackville.

'Good. That's it in a nutshell.'

'But does it mean, Father, that if you're given absolution the sin is completely forgiven?' asked Benjamin.

'Yes. But it does not of course wash away the sin itself. What's done is done. Absolution only washes away the guilt due to sin. It is God's selfless act of forgiveness. And that is what love, real love, is.'

'Does God love everybody?' asked Arthur, spilling tea into his saucer. 'Can he forgive everybody in the world?'

'Of course, Arthur. But it is up to the individual to make himself available to this forgiving love. The sinner must be truly contrite. That is to say, he has a heartfelt sorrow and detestation of the sin he has committed.'

'But—' interrupted Manning.

'I haven't finished yet. What I am going to say is very important. Besides being sorry he must have a firm resolve not to sin again.' Mary knocked and entered.

'I'll just clear away now, Father.'

'Come on everyone, let's continue in the chapel.' The group said their grace privately, made the sign of the cross and left the room for Mary to clean. In the sacristy they passed Father Pollard who was preparing the vestments with due ceremony for another Mass the next day.

'When does the celebrant wear red?' asked Goddard as the procession moved through towards the chapel.

'A martyr's feast day,' said Benjamin.

'Indeed Benjamin is right. Red vestments are the colour of a martyr's feast day. Red for the blood shed in Christ's name.' Goddard and his retinue entered the chapel. The honey-stone interior was wild with glittering summer morning light. In obvious high spirits, Goddard burst into song, accompanying the hymn that Father Henry was teaching Reiner on the organ. Despite a few hidden smirks, some of the boys joined him.

> 'Faith of our Fathers living still in spite of
>   dungeon fire and sword—
> Oh how our hearts beat high with joy,
> Whenever we hear that glorious word.
> Faith of our Fathers living still
> We will be true to thee till death.
> We will be true to thee till death.'

The cavalcade turned down the centre aisle and crossed to the alcoves at the side of the church where the confessionals were located. Even on that brilliant morning this area remained cool and shaded. As usual in the chapel, conversations were conducted in a reverent whispered tone, whatever the subject.

'Why is it all done in secret, Father?' asked Dowd.

'It's obvious, idiot. Who'd confess if the neighbours knew what you'd been up to?' quipped Benjamin. Goddard smiled indulgently.

'Benji's right. That certainly is one reason, though it's not the whole picture. When you confess to a priest in the confessional, you are not telling the priest, rather, through him you are speaking directly to God. What you say is a matter between you and God and no one else. The priest is God's ear, if you like. What he hears is between you and God, therefore he is obliged to keep whatever is confessed secret—forever.

'Look,' he continued, opening a cubicle, 'between the voice of the penitent and the listening ear of the confessor is this grille or screen. This simple device helps retain the anonymity necessary for this act.'

'It must be easier to talk about really bad sins if the priest is hidden,' said Cawley.

'Yes. It reminds the person he's really confessing to God,' said Benji, directly to Goddard.

'Very good,' smiled the priest, 'that is the crux of our discussion. For the priest is here only as an intermediary, the middle-man between the penitent and Almighty God. It is for this reason, incidentally, that the priest is bound to secrecy.'

A hand shot up to question. 'Surely, Father, there must be some circumstances in which he's obliged to tell what he's heard?'

'Can anyone answer Dominic's question?' asked the priest, looking at his disciples. The boys, who had long been drilled in the basic lessons of confession answered that the secrecy of the confessional was inviolate. It was a fact accepted without question.

'Exactly. There are no circumstances in which the seal of the confession can be broken. No information of any kind can be passed on by the priest. The silence of the confessional is absolute. Take an extreme example. If I told my confessor I was strongly tempted to murder someone—and if you don't stop yawning Arthur, I may carry out my threat.'

'That'd be no great loss,' mumbled Manning. Benjamin smiled his agreement. Arthur shifted his weight from one leg to the other and smiled weakly.

Goddard resumed, 'A confessor is absolutely forbidden to speak or act upon the information he has heard in the confessional because of his privileged position—the servant of God is bound to silence in speech and action. In the extreme case I mentioned—and I was only joking, Arthur—the confessor, though he could do nothing about my threat, would no doubt warn me I was putting my soul in a perilous position.'

Benjamin asked under what circumstances any privy information could be discussed between priest and penitent.

'Well,' said Goddard guardedly, 'the penitent in an extraordinary circumstance may give the priest permission to discuss what was said in the confessional, but even then the priest is bound to remain silent.' Arthur put up his hand.

'Father,' he said, 'suppose the priest did break the seal? What if he is so disturbed by what he has heard he has to tell another priest . . .'

'Arthur, Father has already said there is no way a priest would tell what he has heard,' chirped Benjamin. Goddard smiled.

Arthur persisted. 'But isn't it humiliating to confess your sins, Father? Isn't it all a bit masochistic?'

Goddard's eyes sparkled. He raised his voice deliberately in the echoing chapel. 'Masochistic. That's a big word for a little

47

boy. What do you know about masochism—or indeed any other ism?'

'I know what it means.'

'Oh you do. That explains it all. You ask foolish questions of me in order that I shall reprove you publicly.' The boys roared their laughing approval. Arthur squirmed.

'All right everyone. I'll see you all in the tutorial room at Lacey House for Latin after the nine o'clock bell.' Goddard swept out of the chapel with Benjamin and Sackville. Arthur hastened to kneel. If Goddard were to see him making a prayerful visit it might make up for the chastisement he had just endured.

Father Pollard was muttering aloud as he changed the flowers on the altar. Stale white and yellow daffodils were being removed from the vases to be replaced by velvet red roses with long thorny stems in preparation for the martyr's feast-day.

High above the altar-piece, the sun was dancing through the coloured glass window—a triptych of the Betrayal. In the left panel, Peter, in a rage, was cutting off the ear of one of the soldiers who had come to the garden to arrest Jesus. In the central panel, there was the mortal kiss of Judas and Christ. The left panel was somewhat less well-lit, being shaded from full light by the branches of a tree outside. Here was the final act, a gesture of reconciliation: Christ healing the bloody ear of the victim.

Arthur bowed his head in prayer.

'To my words give ear, O Lord
Give heed to my groan
Attend to the sound of my cries
My King, My God
It is you whom I invoke, O Lord
To my words give ear.'

'In the name of the Father, and of the Son, and of the Holy Spirit, Amen. Good morning, be seated ... silently. Dowd, you can't sit without scraping your chair, can you? As it is such a wonderful day let us get this over with as quickly and painlessly as possible. I speak of the excruciatingly joyful exercise of Latin translation.'

48

A series of groans echoed round the classroom. Goddard, still in a good mood, playfully extended the agony.

'Now, David—or perhaps Dominique—No, David. Why don't you open the Gallic war reporting. The rest of you, pick up those sheets in front of you. I am sure you recognise the extract. Where have you seen it before?'

'In the test question,' said David rather miserably.

'Indeed. The very thing. I have spent the last night, while you were safe and warm in your beds, correcting your translations of this extract. But more of that later,' the priest threatened.

'Did you mark it hard?' asked Arthur.

'I marked the efforts according to their worth.'

Benjamin whispered to Hardy, 'He's in too good a mood. Our answers must have been terrible.'

David began to translate but Goddard interrupted, 'Stand up, David. Share your voice.' He began again.

'Caesar urged his men to make all speed through the ... through the valley ...' Goddard had begun a slow perambulation, weaving in and out of the desks.

'Gorge or defile. A valley is too broad a place.' David nodded and continued, 'To make all speed through the defile or gorge—'

'One will do, it's either one or the other ...'

'Gorge—'

'Good choice, makes it more dramatic.'

'... in order that they might reach the safety of the hills before the night fell.' Goddard was now in front of the standing boy.

'Good ... crisp, efficient. Why you couldn't have translated as well as that in the test remains a mystery to me. Now, who shall give us the next thrilling instalment?' David sat, revealing Arthur Dyson immediately behind him.

'Arthur. Why don't you?'

Arthur stood, knocking a large folder off the desk. There was laughter from the other boys. Goddard, whose back was turned, continued to walk towards the front of the room. In his effort to retrieve the folder, Arthur dislodged a ruler and some pencils and sent them clattering to the floor. Goddard still did not turn round.

'Are we to have sound effects with your reading, Arthur?'

'No, Father.' He retrieved his fallen papers and pencils but Benjamin's foot was firmly on the ruler, so that was out of reach. Arthur stood and stared at the printed sheet for a full minute. Goddard, now standing framed by the blackboard, turned to face him, waiting for him to speak. Still, Arthur did not speak. Goddard fingered the pile of corrected answer booklets, picked out what was obviously Arthur's effort, and placed it open on the master's desk.

At last, with difficulty, Arthur began. 'But circumstances were found to ... but circumstances were found to ...' He looked helplessly at the page, his face screwing into difficult little lines, signalling the enormity of the effort that was going into his translation.

'Yes, Arthur?' came Goddard's chilly voice.

'I'm not sure, Father.'

Goddard looked at the answer booklet in front of him.

'Impedire. Surely you get an inkling of the meaning from the sound. Impedire. Listen to the sound.' Goddard repeated it, heavily emphasising the English connotation in the word.

'Impedire,' he said. 'Repeat it after me—impedire.'

'Impedire,' replied Arthur.

'Say it again.'

'Impedire.'

'Well—impedire!'

This only served to fluster Arthur and impede any chance he had of taking a guess at the word's meaning.

'Oh, tell him, for goodness sake. Benji.'

'Impede, Arthur.'

'Impede, Father,' echoed Arthur bleakly.

'Yes. Literally, to entangle the feet. To hinder, to obstruct. Hence—impede. Impedire. To impede. Not wholly surprising, is it?'

'No, Father,' agreed Arthur, in a small quiet voice.

'No. Well get on with it and stop impeding the progress of this lesson.' Arthur looked around at the rest of the boys, most of whom were laughing. He laughed with them.

'Come on, that's enough,' said Goddard. Arthur obediently returned to his labour, but it was hopeless.

'To impede their march and hold them quietly ...'

'What does that mean, Dyson?'

'I don't know, Father.'

'You don't know, Father.' Goddard's anger was swift and sudden, though the voice remained quietly incisive. 'You don't know, Father. Well I know a bone lazy stupid boy when I see one. You just haven't prepared the work, that's it, isn't it?'

'No, Father, I did it Father, truly.'

'Don't add deceit to sloth. Some boys are idle, some are foolish, but I have never met any boy quite as indolent or doltish as you. You will stay indoors this afternoon and translate this whole section into perfect English. Furthermore, you will rewrite the whole of your examination answer in a tidy and respectable form. Be warned, I will not accept pages of grubby hieroglyphics like these.' He dangled Arthur's answer booklet before him as though it were diseased.

'But Father, I did do the work. I read all about Roman strategy. I studied their uniforms. I even drew some.'

'Sit down,' bellowed the priest.

Arthur sat, the blast of the voice reddening his face. As he did so, the rest of the class rose. Arthur and Goddard simultaneously followed suit as Father Rivers wandered into the classroom.

'Good morning, Father Goddard, good morning, gentlemen.' A murmur of good mornings from the boys was cut with Goddard's crisp greeting. Father Rivers waved the boys back to their seats. 'I'm just strolling about, putting my head into classrooms to see how things are progressing.'

'In here we are progressing slowly. There are serious impediments, Father.'

'What is our subject this morning?'

'Latin translation,' replied Sackville, 'Caesar's Gallic Wars.'

'Ah. Big Julie meets the Flying Frogs, as I once heard it described by a boy in this school.'

'These are the most recent test results, Father,' said Goddard, handing him a blue sheet of marks.

'32% ... is that top? Oh ... well done Raphaels. Sackville 29%. Hardy 26. Stanfield 25% David ... 22. Oh dear. Not very good, Nick, 12. Arthur 8. What an abyss of achievement!'

'They were particularly difficult pieces I chose for the test, Father, but I didn't quite expect these results,' said Goddard.

'Has anyone anything to say for himself?' enquired the principal.

'I don't like Latin, Father. It doesn't agree with me,' offered Manning.

'Carbohydrates don't seem to agree with you but that doesn't stop you liking to ingest them in vast quantities,' snapped Goddard.

'I am sure Father Goddard has said this,' resumed Rivers, 'but I'll repeat it now. Ancient languages are the scabbard which hold the mind's sword. The origins of our words are so important ...' Benjamin spoke up as the old priest spluttered on.

'I can't see the point, Father, of studying something we no longer use, even in the Mass.'

Father Rivers smiled indulgently. He mourned the passing of the Latin Mass. 'The laity may not have to know Latin ... Benjamin, isn't it? ... but I'm afraid the pro's are expected to. You see, these old languages are not dead. They live on in the form of our modern words. They enhance our precise understanding of what we say. They aid our self-expression.'

Goddard thinly smiled his interruption. 'I feel that Benjamin's examination marks scarcely do him justice, Father. As a matter of fact he was just about to translate when you arrived. Perhaps you would care to stay and ... ?'

'By all means. Pray continue.' Father Rivers made his way to the spare seat near Arthur Dyson, while Goddard resumed his position on the podium at the front of the classroom.

'All right, Benjamin, take it from where Arthur left off. And do try and make the text work in English.'

Benjamin stood and angled his attention across the room to take in Father Rivers on his left and Father Goddard on his right. He translated effortlessly.

'They found—that's the Romans, Father,' he informed the beaming Father Rivers, 'found that circumstances were against them and their progress was impeded.'

Goddard smiled reassuringly at him and indicated that the others should take note of Benjamin's reading. Thus encouraged, Benjamin launched into the next phrase.

'They realised that if they were to get into a position to bump off the Gauls, they'd better pull their fingers out p.d.q.'

The class broke into uproar. Father Rivers continued to beam appreciatively. He looked to Goddard—whose face had hardened into granite.

'What do you think you're doing?'

'I'm just trying to make the text work in English as you said.'

'Don't be impertinent.'

'I'm not, Father. The Duke of Edinburgh himself used the phrase in public . . .'

'Further impertinence! You will keep Arthur company in detention this afternoon, and write out in perfect English a translation of the text I shall give you. You shall head the translation I shall not use slang in my translation.'

Benjamin stood, ashen-faced. He was quite unused to public reprimands from Goddard. Bewildered, he fingered the leaves of paper on his desk. Father Rivers, who was quite amused by the joke, found Goddard's heavy reprimand unwarranted but was powerless to subvert any priest's authority in the classroom. He turned to Benjamin and asked kindly, 'You say the Duke of Edinburgh uses that expression?'

Benjamin nodded abstractedly. His gaze was still on Father Goddard.

'Well Benjamin, I can only say that this is a valuable lesson in not putting your trust in princes.' He picked up one of the drawings of Roman soldiers that Arthur had deliberately placed on view before him.

'What a splendid sketch. Your own work?'

'Yes, Father,' stammered Arthur, 'and here is a siege ramp. I took the idea from a picture I saw in the library, and I'm going to try and make a model to present to the school . . .'

'God bless you,' interrupted Father Rivers.

'Perhaps you'd like to give Father Rivers a sample of your Latin translation, Arthur,' said Goddard coldly.

Arthur faltered briefly, then stood. Father Rivers had wandered across the room, greeting other boys.

'Father, before translating the text, I'd really like to show all the research I've done on the siege ramps.'

'Another time, Arthur. When you've completed your model you can give a brief dissertation.'

'But Father . . .'

'Dyson—translate!'

'Yes Father. They enclosed themselves in earthworks twelve feet high. This position angered the Romans—Father, what would you have done in that situation?'

53

'Dyson. Translate. This is not a discussion of strategy but a simple exercise in translation.'

'I know, Father, but they could build a siege ramp like the one you told us about at Maseda.'

'Hic constitutis rebus, nactus ... Come Dyson. Nactus?'

'Nactus—from Nancisor,' helped Father Rivers.

'I'm sorry, I don't know,' replied Arthur, stumblingly.

'No. I daresay you don't. Your head is full of siege ramps. A dangerous impediment to the satisfactory translation of a straightforward piece of Latin,' said Goddard.

But Arthur found a most unexpected defender, Benjamin spoke up. 'But surely Arthur's right about siege ramps. This second passage is about the North African Wars, where siege ramps were used.'

For a moment Goddard was silent, framing a tactical response to this novel situation, then smoothly replied, 'Although both passages deal with some aspect of strategy, the techniques you describe, and which hold such a fascination for Arthur, had not been developed in 57 B.C.'

Father Rivers walked across to Goddard. 'Well, I'll leave you to the strategy of a morning of Latin, Father.'

Goddard accompanied the older priest to the door. In the relative privacy of the doorway Father Rivers turned to face him. 'Father Moore has decided not to involve the police in last night's incident. Not very much was stolen.'

'But Father, it may have been one incident in a spree of break-ins. The police should be informed.'

'Well, Father Moore feels that it is a minor incident, and could very well be one of the boys.'

'Hardly likely ... I'll speak to Father Moore.'

'Oh, by the way, I have employed a lad to help out around the place for the day. He will work mainly in the grounds. Father Pollard needs some things to be carried up from the Rivers was genuinely quaint, or merely senile. 'A gypsy?'

Goddard looked puzzled. He was never sure whether Father Rivers was genuinely quaint, or merely senile. 'A gypsy?'

'Well, not really a gypsy. I just called him that because he wears a little gold earring.'

Goddard was scandalised. 'An earring!'

'Yes. That's him down there.'

Across the courtyard, behind the chapel, Goddard could

only see Father Pollard, indicating to someone down in the
cellars. Suddenly, from beneath the chapel, out of the hole in
the ground which served as a cellar door, emerged Blakey. He
was stripped to the waist, his hair tied back in a tail by a piece
of beaded leather. From his broad belt hung a bright red cotton
T-shirt. The powerfully built body contrasted dramatically
with the frail grey frame of Father Pollard. They were laughing
and talking, clearly enjoying each other's company. Goddard's
eyes filled with rage, it seemed the whole morning was con-
spiring against him.

Father Rivers wandered off down the corridor, tapped on
another classroom door, and entered. Goddard returned to his
own class, who abruptly lapsed into silence.

'Right. We'll finish this work. The final extract is from a
section of the Gallic Wars. Raphaels. Translate.'

The Welsh-Italian linguist stood and translated the passage
perfectly. 'They realised that if they were ever to get into a
position to destroy the enemy they had better change their
tactics with the utmost celerity. Caesar ordered his forces to
regroup and retreat some distance from where they stood.
Here there were many trees where they found protection from
the eyes of the enemy.'

After ten minutes or so, Arthur broke the silence. 'Benji ...
Benji ... Thanks for siding with me against God.' Benjamin
didn't answer.

Arthur returned to the dreary task of translation. Benjamin
was staring out at the thin line of boys making their way
across the playing fields towards Basket Wood. He knew that
if he'd been running that afternoon, he would have set a pace
ahead of the rest and headed deeper into the wood to find the
intruder. He hoped they would not find any evidence of his
camp. If Sackville or Hardy did, all would be lost, for they
would report the alien presence to Goddard and Blakey
would be moved on.

Suddenly the green fields and woodscape melted into a blur.
Water streamed down the glass to reveal Blakey stretched
across it atop a ladder. He began vigorously washing the window, making a violent squeaking with the chamois-leather.
He mouthed a cheering hello to Benjamin. Benjamin smiled
back. Whether he was recognised from the night before or not,

Benji couldn't be sure, for Blakey just went on rubbing the glass. Arthur turned and caught sight of him.

'Who's that?' he squeaked, as though he had received a rather painful visitation from the Holy Ghost. 'Benjamin! It's the bike-rider. What's he doing here?'

'Be quiet. You and I are in enough trouble already.'

'I'll go and get Father.'

'Arthur, sit down . . . please!'

'I'd better tell Father.'

'No, don't. I think God must have given him an odd job after all.' Arthur was not convinced but nonetheless returned to his place. Benji lifted his hair at the front to display the small cut on his forehead. Still Blakey gave no sign of recognition. Trying not to arouse Arthur's curiosity any further, Benji surreptitiously hauled his tie over his shoulder, opened his shirt, and showed the bruised chest to the man outside. Again he lifted his hair, hoping Blakey would see the scars and recognise him.

Blakey playfully imitated his actions. He then clutched his chest in mock pain. Benjamin looked round, to find Arthur staring with great curiosity at this mime. He returned to face Blakey.

'You know who I am?' he mouthed, pointing at the man. For a moment there was no reply. Benjamin urgently repeated the signal.

'You and me . . .' His left and right hand fought a mock battle. Blakey looked, then spat violently at him, the saliva oozing down the glass. He wiped it away with the wet chammy and smiled broadly. Benji smiled back. Blakey indicated that Arthur was watching. In fact, Arthur could vaguely see the whole ritual Benji was performing reflected in the window. Benji saw that his head and shoulders were reflected where Blakey's stomach darkened the glass.

Arthur didn't speak. He was concentrating on the elaborate mime that Blakey had begun. He pretended to catch the freckles on his shoulders and chest as if they were gnats, then pinned them to the window with spit. Arthur and Benji broke into laughter as the game accelerated and became more lunatic. Not only his freckles, but now his hair, his eyes, his nose, his mouth, now his ears, his nipples, his navel—he transposed his whole body onto the glass to create some bizarre imagined stained-glass mural composed of living elements of flesh. The boys marvelled. Arthur got up from his appointed place and came across to watch the enchanter more closely.

When Blakey had exhausted all the possibilities of the game, he leant over and kissed the imaginary figure. The boys laughed as Blakey made frantic gestures as if his tongue had become stuck to the glass. Then he picked up a soapy sponge and splashed it violently over the pane, erasing the fantasy for ever. His sudden industry indicated that someone had arrived at the foot of the ladder.

'I'll just finish this one and come down,' he called. The words washed the game away completely and he disappeared from view.

After a moment, Benjamin turned to Arthur. His tone was sweet and inviting. 'Let's keep this a secret—between ourselves.'

'What, the man carrying on like that?'

'Come on, Arthur, you laughed.'

'He was funny.'

'Listen Arthur . . . if you keep this a secret between us, I'll tell you something about me. Something I would only ever tell to my most trusted friend.'

'What?' gasped Arthur, the promise of trusted friendship from Benjamin Stanfield being like a glimpse of heaven. 'Benji, you know you can trust me. I always wanted to be good friends with you.'

'Arthur. I could hear your voice all along the corridors. Is there any reason for talking?' rasped Goddard.

'No Father.'

Benjamin looked straight at Arthur.

'Were you talking Stanfield?'

'Benji wasn't talking Father, it was only me, I was trying to make him talk . . .' said Arthur.

'I'll have to separate you, then. Benjamin, you will continue your detention in the dormitory. Arthur will remain here.'

Benjamin picked up his work-book and left. Arthur looked at him for some reassurance, but none came. He presumed his reward would come in less dangerous circumstances. Goddard walked across to the window.

'What is all this water, Dyson?'

'Some man is cleaning the windows, Father. I just heard the squeaking noise and was asking Benjamin what it was when you came in.'

'Did Stanfield communicate with the fellow?'

'No Father. I'm not sure, really, I was facing away from the window.'

'Yes. Well, move your work over here, you can sit at this desk. If that fellow comes back you must not speak to him. He's a bad element. I do not know whatever possessed Father Rivers to employ him.'

'Is he the same man from yesterday, Father, the one you scared away?'

'That's no concern of yours.'

Goddard did not knock but stormed into Father Moore's office. Father Keenan, who had dropped in for a chat, hailed him cheerily, but the words died on his lips as Goddard cut in, 'Keenan, will you excuse us a moment. I have urgent business with Moore.' Father Keenan stood and left without another word.

Goddard went into action. 'Michael, can you explain to me why you allowed the head to employ that fellow?'

'What fellow?'

'The gypsy. That creature with the motor-cycle I sent packing yesterday is at present running about the school, disrupting the place and disturbing my boys.'

'Richard, I don't know anything about him. You'd better talk to the Head. I believe he is only here for the day and working in return for a meal.'

'He's already had one free meal on us. I am absolutely certain he is the one who broke in last night.'

'There is no proof of that. Besides, he wouldn't dare show his face again if that were the case.'

'Michael, we are dealing with a criminal element. I can tell them a mile off.'

Father Rivers came into the office. 'Oh Richard, come in and have some tea.'

'Father, I'll come in, but not for tea. I must talk to you about this fellow you employed.'

'Oh, Blakey, Blake ... something. Charles is his Christian name. Although one never knows these days if Christian is the precise way of describing a forename. Come in, Richard. I want a chat.'

Goddard scowled at Father Moore as if he was in some way responsible for the whole business, and then followed Father Rivers into the beautiful old sitting room that formed the principal's office.

In contrast to the functional wood-panelling and beige stone of the outer office, here all was burgundy and charcoal. A large desk dominated the room in the same way an ornate altar does a simple stone chapel. It was a magnificent carved table from Andalusia, bulls-blood wood with leather writing accoutrements. The chair was as grand as a bishop's throne, almost too grand for the head of a middle-sized boys' school. Above it hung an old ebony crucifix on which an ivory Christ suffered. One of its legs had been broken and repaired with far too much glue, so besides the conventional wounds of the faith, there was one large fracture of the thigh.

When Goddard assumed the principal's seat this crucifix, the only precious personal property of Father Rivers, would be removed and Goddard's own personal talisman would stand in its place. Above the chair was a painting of the Sacred Heart.

Father Rivers poured tea with all the deliberation of a new altar-boy filling the chalice at Mass. Goddard fingered the rosary-beads in his pocket, repeating the 'Hail Marys' instead of counting to ten. Father Rivers spoke first.

'I must say I thought you were unnecessarily hard on young ... Banfield.'

'Stanfield,' corrected Goddard.

'Yes, you were unnecessarily hard on him this morning. The joke was harmless enough.'

'It was the most blatant impertinence.'

'Oh, come, Richard, he was just showing off in front of me.'

'I know Benjamin, Father. I spend most of my waking hours with the boys. He is a brilliant and imaginative fellow but cursed with a trickster sense of humour which he nourishes with vulgar exhibitionism such as we saw this morning. That kind of boy needs careful guidance and a firm reining-in. For his own sake.'

'You are very ambitious for Benjamin.'

'Not just for Benjamin. I hope I am ambitious for all the boys in my care.'

'Just the sentiments I like to hear from one who will succeed me as Principal—yes, it's been confirmed by the Director-General, you begin next term. Moore will remain the Administrator and Bursar, and perhaps Keenan or young Walsh shall take over Lacey House.'

'My wish is to stay a House-Master.'

'I don't think that's wise, Richard. You are taking too much on yourself already. I am absolutely convinced your snap reprimand of Benjamin is the result of all this extra work—no, don't look at me like that—we are very old acquaintances and despite a lot of illness in recent years some of the grey matter is still functional. Have a fish paste sandwich, Hoskins gets moody if they aren't all eaten up.'

Goddard declined and continued through another decade of the rosary.

'You know, Richard,' Father Rivers continued, 'at times you and Moore and Hoskins treat me like a demented old mother that they don't have the heart to send to a home.'

If he hadn't been clenching his teeth to murmur the preparatory 'Our Father' to the next decade of the rosary, Goddard's jaw would have fallen open in amazement. Father Rivers had never been an intimate friend of his. He was an academic appointed to the position by the then Director-General after a stroke; he had remained aloof to the career priests at the school. This burst of intimacy was quite uncharacteristic. Goddard took his fingers from the beads and smoothed down the wide sash from off his lap until it dangled onto the floor. He even accepted a fish-paste sandwich, took a token bite, and placed the remains on his saucer. Rivers went on.

'You know, perhaps it is all illusory, what we teach—or the emphasis of our teaching, at least. Divinity, dead languages. I have been doing it on and off for forty years, and I still think, sometimes, we'd be better off teaching them things which would be more useful in the modern world, providing them with equipment. I don't know—sex . . . cooking . . .'

Goddard didn't reply immediately, but thought to himself, 'Oh. So it's that mood this afternoon.'

'Oh, come, like most of us I was deeply distressed at the

modernisation of the ritual—something of the mystery was lost.'

Goddard was not in the mood for a rambling discussion about the liturgy between sips of lapsang souchong.

'You know as well as I do, Father, that our boys receive a total education here. Sommerbury is a truly Catholic educational institution; and you know when I say Catholic I mean universal—the precise meaning of the word. Universal, and nothing truly human can be alien to it.'

'I wonder, Richard, I wonder. The slowness of my dying has created in me more doubt, no, uncertainty than I ever managed to contrive in any of the intellectual excesses I indulged in. I thought I could talk to you about it.'

'Surely, Father, these issues are more for your confessor, the Father Superior, and not me.'

'Maybe so—but the heir apparent must have some idea of the thorns in the crown before he puts it on.'

Goddard winced. Arthur Dyson at his worst could not have bettered the metaphor. 'Father, I believe what you are saying to me is relevant, in the sense that we have to find the contemporary despair and the contemporary aspiration in ourselves, or we can't possibly have anything to say to anybody else.' There was a long silence. Goddard hoped he had terminated the meeting. Father Rivers continued to sip his weak black tea. Goddard took a deep breath and went on picking tiny crumbs off his soutane, dropping them absent-mindedly onto the ash-grey floor as he spoke.

'God is liberal, and therefore our work is to liberate—to set people free—to resolve for our boys those conflicts which turn men to despair in later life. What is any education worth without the realization that *truth* is bigger than oneself, and that certainty lies beyond rational explanation?'

Rivers looked up, and spoke gently and sincerely. 'I only hope the boys have some real idea of what you are trying to do for them.'

'Well, as you know, it is difficult for young people to realize that they are being given the key to life's biggest prison—because they don't suspect it even exists yet. Inhibition, loneliness, hesitancy—a very real prison.'

'Orthodox religion . . . can be a cell.' Father Rivers stared at him. 'Or I should say, orthodoxy of any form.'

Goddard didn't bother to reply. Jesuits in the intellectual dance begin from an attitude of unbelieving, an attitude in which they will use any stigma to beat a dogma. Goddard knew all the tricks and did not care to be partnered by a man whose mind he felt was fading like an old radio, all static, dying phases, poor reception.

'Father, the reason I came to see you is that I feel that your gypsy lad is of a criminal element prepared to disrupt anything.'

Rivers looked puzzled. He wasn't aware the subject had changed. 'Really! What can you mean!'

'Exactly what I say, Father. It is my genuine belief that he is responsible for last night's theft . . .'

'Oh come now, he wouldn't be here today . . .'

'He was here yesterday and I sent him packing for the very reason that I know his type.'

'Well, well. The lad is going this afternoon. His work is finished.'

Father Moore came in with Father Rivers' afternoon papers. 'Oh, Richard, that fellow you were so anxious about has left. I offered him a meal for the work but he said that Father Pollard had taken care of payment.'

'What does that mean?'

'Well it seems he gave him some relic he bought in Rome— a chip of bone of Maria Goretti mounted in a cross. The fellow was absolutely delighted.'

'Well he's gone then.'

'Yes, Father Goddard—was there some trouble?' inquired Moore.

Goddard stood. 'Thank you for the tea, Father Rivers. Will you excuse me?'

'Of course Richard. You know, weighing all this up, it seems a little disproportionate to me. You just said that Catholic is universal, and nothing truly human can be alien to it. Unless of course you don't regard this gypsy as being human.'

'For the purpose of discipline I am quite prepared to regard him as an alien being, but I do feel that gypsy is a highly romantic title for a common or garden thug.' Goddard swept out.

My mother said
That I never should
Play with the gypsies
In the wood.
My father said
That if I did
He'd bang my head
With the teapot lid

Benjamin broke into a run as soon as he was out of the dormitory. He would have run inside too if it wasn't strictly against the rules. He had put the detention papers under the door of Goddard's study with a sincere note of apology clipped to their front. The mellow honey-coloured stone sped past him. He took no notice of a shout of greeting from Sackville and the others returning from their cross-country. He did take time to wave at poor Arthur incarcerated in the tower by the library—besides, the slight detour allowed him to check whether Blakey was still around.

In case anyone was watching him he took the conventional cross-country route that followed the tangled ancient path across by the trees. Once he had reached those trees he could safely make his way into Basket Wood to seek out Blakey.

Benji enjoyed pushing himself in these runs, pumping the air into his lungs, sensing the strain in his body. At the top of the hill he stopped and flexed his chest-muscles to reawaken the pain of the bruising from the night before, then stooped to adjust his socks.

The day was sunny and hot, and there, above Sommerbury, infinitely peaceful. As far as the eye could see, the countryside stretched away, folded and tucked into valleys and hills, green and brown and splashes of ochre, and the land held him with an ageless mystery. For a moment, the singing of a spring afternoon was joined by the faint cascades of the school choir. 'Sleepers Awake'.

Benjamin took off his wet, clinging singlet, wiped his face and armpits, and hooked it through the hitch-tag on his running shorts, the green scapula a splash of colour against his chest. It was a very small act of defiance. Athletes were forbidden to appear except in full kit. Benjamin ran down the hill into the tangled wood.

It did not take long to find the camp. He could hear the guitar, and followed its song to the river, but when he came close upon it, he was confused—there seemed to be no sign of Blakey or his camp. This was also a little cheering, for it made him certain that the other runners could not have discovered it. The sound stopped. A movement in the trees and he crouched down hoping not to be seen. Another movement directly before him among the exposed roots of the large tree where Blakey had made his camp. Benjamin held his breath as the curly head emerged from beneath the camouflaging leaves at his feet. Blakey dragged a hammock across the clearing. While he was tying the rope, Benjamin drew from his sock a small metal slingshot he had taped to his leg. He felt around for a stone, loaded his weapon, and took careful aim. Blakey, bending down to pick up the other rope, was an ideal target. The missile connected. Blakey bellowed and danced madly about holding his wounded behind. Benjamin leaped out from behind the tree and shouted.

'You're trespassing, gyppo.'

'You little prick,' screamed Blakey, and hurled a rock at him. Benjamin ducked and darted down the ridge into the clearing.

'Pays you for last night.'

'I didn't hurt you, man.'

'I didn't tell anyone about you stealing, breaking and entering.'

'So what you want? A fuckin' medal?'

In the daylight, Benjamin could see his night-foe was not the giant he had imagined. In fact, he was not much taller than himself. 'I see you already have a medal.'

Blakey picked up the cross dangling outside the open shirt. 'Yeh, the old man gave it to me—Father Pollard. Know him? Yeh, he told me it had a chip of the breast-bone of some saint or something.'

Benjamin remained silent and kept his distance in case Blakey made any attempt to pay back the stinging insult. Blakey went on, 'I told him how I went to a Catholic school.'

'Did you?'

'What?'

'Go to a Catholic school?'

'Eh! Come over here, sit down.' An audience had been granted in the lair of the Woodland King. Blakey offered Benjamin a hand-rolled cigarette. Benjamin declined. 'Pipe of peace, boy. Well, it's for you.' Again Benjamin shook his head. 'Frightened you'll catch something?'

'I don't smoke.'

Blakey laughed. Benjamin winced a little at the lie. He did sound rather prissy. Blakey shrugged, lit the cigarette, completed tying the hammock and climbed into it. Benjamin, still at a safe distance, moved across to the grotto where Blakey housed his bike. After a while, Blakey spoke, quite amiably. 'I stopped in your Holy City last year—Rome. Been there? Amazing, absolutely amazing place. Rich, man, rich stuff. Paintings, maps, sculpture, worth millions. A fortune. Made me wonder, though, 'cos the parish priest in our wee village, one winter when I was little, couldn't afford a sack of coal for a fire. Don't seem right, don't you think?'

Benjamin turned to him. He hadn't heard much of what he'd been saying. He was totally absorbed by the bike.

'How fast does it go?' he asked, caressing the long frame.

'A ton.'

'Come off it—down a steep hill with a gale behind you.'

'Not built for speed lad, it's a cruiser. I've been to Iran on that bike—Shiraz. You been to Iran?'

'I've never been anywhere.'

There was a long silence. Blakey looked at him hard, dragged on the smoke, picked a few shreds of tobacco off his tongue, and looked away. Benjamin was embarrassed by that response. He was ashamed of the awkward, rather childish way he had introduced himself. It seemed foolish now. All would have been easier if the painful shot had infuriated him and set them to fighting again, but the quiet, almost magnanimous way in which the intruder had invited him to look around this part of the wood, as if it were his own, showed up Benji's childishness. The wild behaviour and devil-may-care attitude that had made him remarkable at the school seemed worthless currency here.

'Do you realise this is private property?' he said tartly.

'Is it? What you doing here then?'

'Well, the school owns most of the land but this part is

65

private. The school has an arrangement with the owners.'

'So do I. What a coincidence. I have an arrangement with the owners.'

'Bullshit.'

'Harsh words, squire. Och, come on, why start getting all uptight about it? I'm doing no harm.'

'I could report you.'

'You'd be the one with a lot of explaining to do.'

'Listen, there's a YMCA about ten miles down the road. Can't you go there?'

'They give me claustrophobia.'

'Are you going to leave or aren't you?'

'Don't be so fuckin' small. You're five minutes out of your nappies and you're talking like a High Court Sheriff. I thought you had balls, guts, a little blood last night. Well I was wrong. You're like the rest, whining little sucker-fish, hiding in the priests' skirts. Piss off. Now! Tell yer old man I sent you.'

Benjamin felt uneasy. He put his singlet back on, leaving it out over his shorts. 'Did you see the others running through here?'

'Yer mates, you mean?' grunted Blakey. 'Yes, I saw them. They told me they've given me till tomorrow or they're going to send the pack out after me. Jesus, what a lot of snots.'

Benjamin circled the hammock. 'I'd better go now.'

'Who's stoppin' you?'

Again Benjamin made movements to leave. 'I thought you were very funny this afternoon, on the ladder at the window.'

'Anyway, what were you doing in that room, you and that other kid. Everyone else was out and about.'

'I was doing detention. For—well, I'm not sure—I was cheeky to God.'

'God?'

'Yes, Father Goddard. That's what we call him.'

'Which one is he?'

'He's the Deputy Head. He's . . .'

'Not that prune-faced undertaker who wouldn't talk to me yesterday? Him?'

'Him.' From the school the bells of the afternoon mass began ringing.

'Bloody bells. Do you do nothing but ring bells at your school?'

'It's the afternoon mass. It's not for the school, it's usually said for people around who want to attend.'

'Listen—here, what's your name?'

'Stanfield.'

'Stanfield,' laughed Blakey. He repeated it several times as if it were unfamiliar, even unpalatable. He mimicked Benjamin until he could see the edge of annoyance he wanted, then warmly said, 'No. Like my name's Charlie ... Charles Blakey is the full monniker. Ah, what's it worth?'

'Benjamin.'

'What a name, Benjamin. A name by any other name keeps you out of harm's way—or something like that. What do your friends call you?'

'Benji.'

'Benji, say a few Hail Marys for a sinner.'

Though by no means devout, Benjamin did not respond well to the slightest sacriligeous inference concerning his faith. 'Do you mean that seriously? Do you want me to pray for you?'

Blakey began to laugh. 'Oh Benji, it's me who should pray for you, you're the one who's dying. You're breathing very thin air up in God's Keep, lad. All that fire and brimstone, all those hosts of heaven, all those days of judgement, all those souls in limbo. It's not true. There's no hell below, no heaven above, no beyond. There's only this here and now. And that God of yours, the black-hearted bastard that shooed me away from your front gate, he knows that. Why would a man want to capture another man's heart with promises of love and life after death when all the love and life is here before your eyes. You have it. I have it. Him, your God, he doesn't, he's empty —and hungry, and you, Benji, he'll feed on. You're the body he wants to eat, yours the blood he wants to drink ...'

Benji interrupted, 'I must go now.' Blakey smiled. He had almost become oblivious to his astounded listener.

'Aye. Go now. Who's stoppin' you?'

'Come again, come again,' he called after the fleeting white figure. Benjamin smiled, though he was shaken by the heretic's sermon.

Goddard had returned to Father Rivers' study before the evening meal. Although he did not apologise for his behaviour

67

that afternoon, he felt some soothing gesture was necessary. He had attended the afternoon mass with the principal. It seemed the correct and fitting gesture that the heir apparent should now be seen with the departing head on every possible occasion.

They crossed the courtyard from the chapel on their way to the masters' common room for a sherry before the evening meal. As they did so, Father Henry passed them, walking across in the opposite direction, accompanied by Arthur, as usual making elaborate gestures in the air.

'Our Father Henry is rather good,' said Rivers, his eyes on the retreating figures.

'Certainly an enthusiast,' replied Goddard, blandly.

'Mind you, English Literature and Music and Drama fellows always have an unfair advantage.'

'Yes,' clipped Goddard, 'their subjects are intrinsically attractive.'

'I always admire him. He has such time and patience for Dyson. The poor child must feel so dreadfully left out most of the time. So much emphasis on the physical side of things. Poor soul, God bless him.'

'I must confess, Father Rivers, that I find him particularly unattractive as a personality.'

'Oh come now . . .'

'No Father, I will not make concessions in his case—it is not his physical affliction—I find him so wanting in spirit.'

'Well, if you say so. But Richard, he does admire you. That is what you must build on.'

Suddenly Goddard stiffened as he glimpsed Benjamin running across the upper fields. Rivers could not see that far.

'What is it, Father?'

'One of the boys—Stanfield—returning from a run.'

'It's a bit late, isn't it, for cross-country?' said Rivers vaguely.

Goddard beckoned Benjamin, who changed tack and raced, sweating and breathless, up the terraces to the two priests.

'Benjamin, the winter curfew is still in operation. In future do not leave it so late to return from a run. You know the wood area is out of bounds after four. It is now nearly a quarter to five.'

'Sorry Father, but I couldn't start till after the detention,

68

and the bruises from last night slowed me down.'

'You were hurt last night?' enquired Father Rivers. God-dard replied, 'Yes, Benjamin fell over pursuing the thief.'

'Ah ... yes ... well done.' Goddard cut in again. 'Quickly Benjamin, inside and prepare for dinner. We should go in now, Father Rivers, the evening chill is not good for anyone.' Benji left, and they walked on.

'Benjamin showed courage in confronting that thief. I think it was an error of judgement to follow him. Nonetheless, it was a brave act.'

'You have great hopes for him, Father,' said Rivers.

'Yes. I'm hoping God has singled him out for a very impor-tant role in this life, a true vocation. He has all the qualities.'

'He'd make a fine priest,' nodded the old man.

'And a splendid Jesuit. I pray for the day.'

Rivers smiled knowingly. 'Yes, Father Goddard, but the aspiration must ignite from within, a vocation cannot be im-posed.' They completed their walk along the covered way in measured silence.

Benjamin would have preferred to sit next to Sackville and the other runners in the dining hall that evening but he found himself wedged between Manning and Gale, with Arthur opposite. Arthur smiled broadly—so broadly that in order to keep the smile alight, he was forced to hold his glasses in place. Benjamin nodded a greeting, but did not care to enter into conversation. He still owed Arthur a secret from the after-noon, but was looking for a way to discourage further intimacy.

'Oh Benji, Benji, when you left the study I found a very interesting book on strategy. There was this thing they in-vented called a panjandrum. It was shaped a bit like a paddle wheel, with a bomb in the middle. The idea was to launch it from a ship and then roll it over the surface of the sea up to the beach, then it exploded.'

'Yes,' smiled Benji, half-heartedly. Arthur leant forward conspiratorially. 'I don't really want to talk about that, Benji, I just did that so the others wouldn't suspect we were dis-cussing anything important.'

'What do you mean, Dyson,' said Benjamin, continuing to eat.

'Well this afternoon you said that we'd be friends and—'

'Shut up,' Benjamin glared at Arthur, emphasising each word.'

'All right, I will Benji.'

The others looked up. Arthur settled back in his seat and remained silent. He took his rebuke as a signal that this was not the time or place for any such discussion.

Later that evening, Arthur came to Benji's bedside. Benjamin, fully dressed, sat reading. 'What is it, Arthur?'

'Benji. What is she like?'

'What?'

'What's she like? You can trust me, I won't tell anybody. It was a girl that kept you late on your run wasn't it? Is she pretty?' Benjamin wasn't slow, but it took some time to make the connection between Arthur's thought and the secret he had been promised.

'Yes, yes, she's all right.'

'Is she a friend of that man at the window?'

'Yes. It's his sister. They're camping in the woods behind the school.'

'That explains why you acted like you knew him.'

'Yes, Arthur, but I couldn't tell you the whole story then because I didn't know I could trust you.'

'Benji, you can trust me, cross my heart and hope to die, you can trust me.' Arthur got up from the bed and drew the curtain closed. He lumped back and sat closer to his new friend.

'Is she blonde, or . . .'

'No, she's got dark hair like her brother, but taller than him with long legs and—' Benjamin cupped his hands to suggest fulsome breasts.

'Bristols!' enthused Arthur.

'They're very free, you know, very open about things.'

Arthur nodded his understanding, took off his glasses and cleaned them vigorously. 'Are you seeing her again tonight?'

Benjamin smiled slyly. 'You are, aren't you? You're lucky, Benji, I'll bet she's in love with you.'

'Well we're getting married tonight in the woods. We're having a gypsy wedding.'

'What's that mean?'

'Well, the bride and bridegroom piss in a bucket.'

70

Arthur pondered this for a moment before putting his glasses back on and cautioning Benjamin. 'You'd better not let Goddard see you.'

'He's going to be best man.'

'Be serious, Benji, there'll be hell to pay if he finds out.'

'He won't, Arthur. Only if you tell him.' Arthur became very solemn. He offered his hand.

'I'm not going to tell him—your secret's safe with me,' he intoned.

'Okay, Arthur. Listen, leave me now. I've got to get myself prepared for the big event.'

'Of course, Benjamin.' He heaved himself up from the bed and made his way out. Benjamin could scarcely contain himself. As soon as Arthur shut the curtain behind him he burst into fits of laughter, burying his head in the pillow for fear Arthur might hear.

Later still, Arthur brought Benjamin a nuptial libation for supper—a steaming hot mug of chocolate. For a wedding gift he brought a large tin of biscuits he normally tried to keep well hidden, though other boys regularly pillaged it. The conversation he had overheard in the games room and around the television had alarmed him and he felt he must warn his new friend about the dangers of the coming enterprise.

'Sackville and Hardy and those said they saw the gypsy boy today in the school grounds. They say they are going to report him.'

Benjamin became alarmed. 'Tonight? Have they done it?'

'No,' answered Arthur. 'Not yet. Goddard's not back from the staff meeting. Benjamin, what will you do? This ruins everything.'

'Arthur, I am going to tell you something now that's just between us. You know the man at the window?'

'Yes,' whispered Arthur.

'Well, he was the one who stole the food—don't interrupt, just listen—it's important. I fought him. Yes, I did meet him. But I let him go, because he was poor and a gypsy and ... well he was only stealing for his family and we're such a rich school. And when Goddard sent him away, he got desperate so he broke in. Believe me, Arthur, I didn't have the heart to report him.'

71

Arthur was silent. The lie had gained such complexity he was finding it difficult to make any sense of it at all.

'But what about his sister?' he finally said.

'There is no sister. I was just kidding you. I'm not marrying anyone tonight. Come on, you made up most of that story yourself. I just agreed with you to protect the real story.'

Arthur wasn't entirely convinced.

'Listen, Arthur, sit down here.' Benjamin patted the bed, inviting the boy to join him. 'It's even more important to me now that you don't tell God. I could get into a lot of trouble. And we have to find some way of stopping the others from telling him. I'm going to him tonight to warn him to leave.'

'Is that the only reason you're going?'

'Yes,' said Benjamin flatly.

'You'd better be careful, Benji, anything might happen.'

'I can look after myself.'

No more was said for a little while; the new friends sat with their biscuits and chocolate. There were so many questions Arthur wanted to ask, his mind browsing through the possibilities of Benjamin's attraction to Blakey. After a while, Benji put his hand on Arthur's shoulder.

'I know what you're thinking Arthur, but it's not like that.' Arthur was still unsure. 'It's all right, I promise you. He's a Catholic, too. He's one of us.' This seemed to settle Arthur for the moment.

'How are we going to stop the others reporting him to God? Most of them will listen to you, but Dowd and that crowd might not. Dowd is always trying to get the better of you.'

'Dowd wasn't on that run this afternoon. Anyway, Dowd is easy to handle. All we have to do is to leave that love letter and a few used Durex for Goddard to find and he'll be out of action.'

'What about Sackville and Hardy?'

'They'll do as I say. I'll just have to remind them that Goddard would like what they do in Basket Wood even less than what I'm planning to do.'

Arthur became uneasy again. The atmosphere had become quite unexpectedly electric as Benjamin catalogued the power he held over every boy in Lacey House.

'What are you planning, Benjamin?'

'Well, I'll tell them that I have some unfinished business

with the thief. That I am going to handle his correction personally.' Benjamin sprang from the bed and opened the drawer of his desk, and drew from within a hollowed-out book he used to hide his valuables. He took out the sling-shot.

'That's mine,' gasped Arthur.

'Yes. I borowed it from your bedroom without asking. I'm sure you don't mind. Besides,' he grinned darkly, 'Goddard told you to get rid of it weeks ago. Come on, Arthur, let's talk to the others. I'm sure you'll help me convince them to keep their mouths shut.'

Several yards from Blakey's campsite, the river had eaten into the bank, making a pool. Here in the moonlight, lay Blakey and Benji. The boy had one arm, sleeve rolled up, trailing in the water. Suddenly he began splashing.

'What are you doing? Settle down,' snapped Blakey.

'Hell, it escaped.'

'Yes of course, you dumpling, it escaped. That's not the way to guddle trout.'

'Guddle,' replied Benji, looking round at his companion, who had just finished gutting the first catch. He laid the fish down on the grass, his brand new knife beside it.

'You tickle 'em—like this—with your pinkie.'

Benji looked at him uncomprehendingly.

'Your pinkie,' repeated Blakey, holding up his little finger.

For well on three minutes they sat in silence. Then Blakey plunged his hands into the water and pulled out a trout. He quickly stunned it with a stone and began to gut it.

'A great art, Benji Stanfield, a poacher's skill.'

Benjamin was watching the dexterity with which the big hands tore out the fish's innards. He admired the manual skill, but more than that he marvelled at the unconscious way the other boy went about his work. There was nothing exhibitionist about him, yet his dexterity was so fascinating. It was not a ritual disembowelling of the fish: nonetheless, it seemed an act of worship.

'Do you ever feel guilty about anything?'

Blakey looked up. He flicked some of the entrails from his fingers and wiped the knife on the grass. 'Now what kind of a question is that?'

'I don't know.' Benji indicated the school. 'Up there they

73

make you feel guilty whatever you do.'

'Too right, Benji boy. They're vultures, that's all. If you stopped apologising for being alive they'd have lost their hold over you. Guilt is a currency like money. Guilt—gold—you can buy and sell people with it. Man is born free and everywhere he's in chains. You know who said that?'

'Rousseau,' answered Benji, almost as if he were answering Goddard in one of their private tutorials.

'Did he?' replied Blakey, genuinely amazed, 'And there was me thinking it was Marx. Here—' he handed Benji the bloody fish—'Take them back to the camp. We'll get a fire going. A midnight feast.' Benji inspected the bloody catch. 'What are you making faces about?'

Benji shrugged and smiled. 'It's just that . . .'

'If you can't catch a live one, you can carry a dead one.' The hunter and his catch moved up from the river and headed towards the camp.

Blakey grilled the trout on an improvised spit while Benjamin lolled sipping Father Henry's whisky. Blakey tested the feast. Ready. Licking the heat from his fingers he handed the stick to Benjamin.

'Thank you,' he replied, rather formally.

'Please—Thank You—You git me, always so polite. You'd say "please" before you stuck a knife into your granny. I bet that first night we met you'd have apologised to me if you'd tore my guts out. I've still got your scratches.'

'Have you ever killed anyone?'

'Sure.' Blakey tossed his curly head with the air of a man who kills at least once a week. 'When I was in the navy—few years now—I took sick on manoeuvres and they flew me home. I went up the stairs and there was the wife in bed with the bloke next door, so I smashed this bottle on the dresser and cut his throat. Then I cut her up—just to teach her a lesson.'

'Did you?'

'Well . . . not exactly like. I went for him but he scampered off down the stairs.' Blakey laughed to himself. 'The wife nearly had a fit. I didn't touch either of them. Why should I? I'd been away for some time. Reckon she'd given me up for lost. No, killing's not my scene.'

'Did you often just go away?'

'Yes, when I finished service, I wandered for a while, sometimes moving around for work, like up on the rigs, or just to pleasure myself, like the trip I told you about.'

'Must be the gypsy in you.'

'Not much real gypsy left in me. On my mother's side I was a real Romany, but the rest is pure tom-cat. You—you must come from a "good background". Well your parents must be spending a thousand quid a term educating you.'

'The fees are paid out of a trust fund my father set up. Is there any whisky left?'

Blakey passed him the bottle. It was empty. 'Never mind, I got a little something stored over here.' He took a small silver hip-flask from one of the panniers on the bike. He picked up another blanket and looked back towards the fire. 'This is how things should be—a fire, a bottle, share and share. If I had money I would give it away. I would. The only pleasure is making others happy. You know the best job I ever had? I was a fortune-teller in the fairground. Doctor Zingora, that was the name. They gave me this cloak with stars and a moon and such on it.' He delved into the bag again and pulled out a satin jacket bearing the celestial design. 'I had this jacket made from it.'

'Put it on, let me see.'

Blakey took off his flying jacket and shirt and donned the moon and stars. 'Well, there I would sit all day in this tent, staring at a crystal ball. I told everybody they'd have good fortune—win on the pools, have great affairs—anything to make them happy. So what? If they walked out with a smile on their faces, I didn't mind what crap I told them.'

'Can you read palms?'

'Sure I can.'

'Read mine.'

Blakey took the hand and scrutinised it. 'Oh aye, oh aye, you're going to live to be eighty.'

'Is that all?'

'No, you'll die in a foreign land.' Blakey made much of the twisting and turning of the hand to catch the firelight. 'You'll marry—three times—and have dozens of children. But then you'll give it all up and become a mission priest in a leper colony.'

'Go on,' Benjamin began to laugh. At first he had hoped

for a serious glimpse into the future, but this did just as well.

'No, no, no more, Zingora is tired. He must rest. Give him the Holy Water of Scotland.' Benjamin laughed as Blakey blessed himself with the whisky, then guzzled it.

'Have you got any money on you?' said Blakey. 'It is customary to cross the palm of the fortune-teller.'

Benjamin looked to the inside pocket of his blazer. 'I've got a pound.'

'That all?'

'Well I only get two pounds for pocket money.'

'It'll do.' He took the pound. 'Don't look worried, Benji, we'll make it a loan. Next winter I'll be back on the rigs. I've got it all worked out. I'll save up and buy a plot of land. Hebrides—no, Mull will be better.'

'Become a farmer?'

'No fuckin' fear,' laughed Blakey, 'I'm no mug. No, I'll install some open-air showers and toilets and let it out for a caravan park. I'll try and start a chain of them. I want to be rich when I'm older. I should make a millionaire by the time I'm fifty.'

'If you keep going the way you are you'll be in jail.'

'So? I've been inside before.'

'What for?'

'Possession.'

'A dangerous weapon?'

Blakey laughed heartily. 'No—dope. The bastards tried to get me for dealing. Listen, if you're ever here when I come back, though, we'll have a little smoking party on the grass—you know what I mean.'

'Are you going?'

'Tomorrow maybe.'

'Where?'

'Llandudno. Thanks for the pound. It'll get me that far.'

'Can I come with you on the pillion?'

'You! Och ... you should see the bike when it's all loaded up, there's scarcely room for me. Besides, there's a pal of mine there who owes me a favour. It could get a bit heavy—know what I mean?'

Benjamin hadn't the slightest idea what he was talking about. Blakey drank some more whisky. 'You going to sleep here? 'Cos I'm going to turn in. There's plenty of room in the guest bedroom.' He pointed to the small enclosure beneath the tree.

'No, I'll get back. I've got to serve the mass tomorrow. I'd better go now.'

'Please yourself. You're welcome to stay. I'm easy.' He stood up and stumbled across the clearing to his sleeping bag. Embroidered on his back was a large mauve Saturn with yellow and orange rings. He took off his shoes and socks, stepped out of his jeans, and without looking at Benji again, disappeared into the womb of the vast tree.

For a moment, Benji was troubled by indecision. There was the excitement of sleeping here with him by the river, pretending (if only for a night) to be a part of this life. On the other hand, he knew his secret was safe with the others, but only for that evening. He decided quickly. It was simple enough. The only real danger to Blakey was Goddard. The only person who could protect Blakey from him was Benji himself. And he could only do that if he kept in Goddard's good books.

Benjamin tiptoed into the dormitory and started to walk to his cubicle. Arthur was awake. 'Benji, where have you been?'

Benjamin signalled him to be quiet. He walked into his own cubicle and began stealthily to undress. Arthur got out of bed, put on his brace and crossed the corridor to Benjamin.

'Come on, tell me.'

'Arthur, for Christ's sake, you'll get us both into trouble. Wait till morning.'

'I couldn't sleep.'

'Shut up. Get back to bed. Everything turned out fine.'

Suddenly the light in Goddard's apartment flicked on. Arthur hurried, with as much speed as he could, back to his own cubicle. The door opened. The priest stood in the shaft of light, wrapped in a dark blue dressing gown. He moved down the corridor to Arthur's cubicle. Arthur was seated on his bed unfastening his brace.

'What are you doing out of bed, Dyson?'

'I was worried Father, I thought I'd left my spare brace in the shower room.'

'It is on the wall by your desk,' said Goddard.

'Yes, I realise that now. I was just dreaming.'

'I don't believe you. Two hundred lines by tomorrow night

77

—"Lying to my teacher threatens salvation". Sometimes, Arthur, I think in your case a good dose of the cane would be the only answer.' Before Arthur could speak, Goddard hissed at him with searing vehemence, 'Get to bed. I'm sick of the sight of you.'

Goddard turned his attention to Benjamin's cubicle, where the curtain was half-open. The boy was apparently asleep. The room was rather untidy for Benjamin, though. His clothes lay tumbled in a heap on the chair and floor. Goddard hesitated, then went in. He picked up a shoe from beneath the desk. It was very muddy. Still wet. He touched the mud, then looked questioningly at the sleeping boy. Goddard never suspected Benjamin of any gross misdemeanour; he couldn't afford to believe Benjamin was anything other than what he thought. But his eyes seemed to be feigning sleep. He put the shoe down, and let the sleeping dog lie.

Part Three

THE CRACKLING OF THORNS

Our Fathers, chained in prison dark.
Were still in heart and conscience free.
How sweet would be their children's fate
If they, like them, could die for thee
Faith of Our Fathers, Holy Faith
We will be true to thee till death.

Apart from an attempt to set fire to Peterson's hair with a cigarette lighter during the offertory, the morning mass passed without incident. Father Goddard attended with Father Rivers, while Father Roberts celebrated the glorious martyrdom of Maria Goretti. At the end of the service, Father Goddard announced that the business of the previous night's staff meeting had not been concluded, and it would therefore continue throughout the morning. The result was that lessons were cancelled and the boys were free to use the day—constructively.

Benjamin was particularly pleased with this development —it meant he would be able to spend time with Blakey in the Wood. His plan was somewhat spoiled by a group meeting of Lacey House, called immediately after breakfast.

The doors to the dormitory were closed and Hardy stood guard. The atmosphere was tense. Sackville spoke first.

'Is he still there, Benji?'

Benjamin became angry immediately. He realised at once that they had been discussing him and his affairs for some time. He turned his coldest, whitest glare onto Arthur, for only he could have revealed the details of his nocturnal outings. Arthur desperately tried to signal his innocence but Benjamin was blind to his protestations.

'It's none of your business.'

'It is our business,' said Cawley. 'We all share the same dorm. If you're found out we'll all suffer.'

'Term's nearly over,' replied Benjamin.

'Come, Benji,' reasoned Sackville, 'there's the break-up picnic.'

'And the results aren't back yet,' joined Manning.

'That's not relevant,' snapped Cawley.

Benji became quiet. He stared hard at his accusing peers. Hardy walked back from the door. 'Listen, Benji, it's nothing to do with the punishment. We like you and, let's face it, he's just rubbish, isn't he?'

'That's right, Benji,' pleaded Arthur, 'I think he could be dangerous.'

'Well, we don't know anything about him,' cautioned Sackville.

'He's probably crawling with fleas,' added Cawley.

'How does he earn his money?' asked Raphaels, usually very quiet in meetings.

'Good point. I'll bet he peddles dope or something.'

'Has he offered any to you?'

'No.' Benjamin snapped, clearly unnerved by his unexpected trial.

'Benji,' said Sackville, putting his arm on his shoulder, 'we're not afraid of God finding out. You can handle that. We're frightened you could, well, go off the rails. I know that sort. They're always hanging about my parent's villa in Algeciras, begging for food. And what they can't beg, they pinch. One of them had this awful skin disease and great scars on his arms from using a dirty syringe. Honestly, Benji, his kind are dangerous.'

Benjamin made neither move nor reply.

Dowd then asked the question he had longed for Sackville or one of the closer brothers to ask.

'Has he touched you up yet? That's probably what he's after.'

In any other circumstance that would have been the point at which Benjamin lost control and smashed his tormentor's face. Instead he simply said 'You don't know anything, any of you.' He shrugged his shoulders from beneath Sackville's hand and left the room to the inevitable buzz of conjecture.

He spent the rest of the morning alone. He wandered into the chapel where he met Father Pollard polishing the wood of the ornate confessional cubicles. He chatted to him amiably about life in general but tried to steer the conversation towards Blakey in particular. The old priest seemed to have a very high opinion of him, admired his forthrightness but admitted he feared for his soul—stung by the worm atheism, Goddard would have said. Father Pollard, however, considered that 'circumstances had caused him to wander in the shadows'.

Benjamin looked at the confessional. As an object, it was a piece of art—high Bavarian Counter-Reformation, ornate almost to the point of vulgarity. It stood in a secluded part of the chapel, the two penintent's boxes embraced the trunk of the pilaster, which housed the confessant's chamber, reached by a small private corridor from the sacristy. In its conceit, it was not unlike the vast oak on the river-bank, with its own natural confessional beneath, where Blakey was at present living. Benjamin's verdant imagination did not overlook the similarity.

He decided that in spite of the dangers of being seen crossing into the wood, in daylight, for no apparent reason, he would visit Blakey at once. But as he made his way across the courtyard, he was intercepted by Paul Cotteril, one of the junior boys.

'Benjamin Stanfield, the head wants a word with you,' announced the herald.

'Now?'

'Yes, he's in his office. He told me to tell you that you were to leave what you were doing and—'

'All right, piss off, I've got the message.'

Benjamin was more curious than angry. What on earth could Rivers want with him? He knocked at the outer office. Father Moore was not there, so he passed to the door of the deep red inner room. He knocked. There was no reply. He knocked again. For a moment he thought that some brats from the junior school were playing a silly practical joke. But he decided to check just in case Rivers had died at his desk while awaiting his arrival.

'Good morning Benji.'

'Good morning Father,' he responded, rather surprised to see Goddard sitting behind the great desk. 'I was called to see the principal.'

'Well, he's here.'

Benjamin smiled disbelievingly—there was no one else in the room.

'Yes, I am the new Head of Sommerbury. Father Rivers announced it to the staff meeting this morning. We've broken for morning tea—I'd like you to join me. A sort of private celebration.'

Benjamin was genuinely delighted for his old master and warmly congratulated him. Goddard accepted his handshake, then ushered him to the sunlit alcove. He sat him down, then opened the big bay windows that led out into the beautiful topiary of the masters' garden with its splendid view of Basket Wood.

Benjamin, the resourceful apprentice, realised that there must be some other reason for this audience. He had been expecting Goddard to strike at any time, but this staging was quite a surprise. Benjamin wondered whether the God Squad had reported him in a body, or if that dreadful weed Arthur had squealed. He was burning to know the author of his betrayal, but he first had to wait through the preliminary ritual. Tea was poured and a sweet almond croissant placed on the plate in front of him.

Goddard intimated that apart from a disappointing Latin result (easily rectified by a supplementary test), his marks were so good he was the dux of the school. This was for Goddard a blessing; to receive the coveted principal's seat at the same time as the decoration of his star pupil. He wasted no time at all introducing the important topic of the priesthood, his most cherished hope for Benjamin's future; how it was the boy's vocation; how he owed it to himself to commit his gifts to the service of God; how he should consider the Jesuit order; how the Director-General, his Father Superior, Dr Mackkerras, already knew all about him, through Goddard. How Benjamin must not rush his decision but must now begin serious thoughts in that direction. And how he should pray for guidance.

'More tea?' Goddard smiled. Benjamin declined, indicating his half-full cup.

'Now you're looking worried again.'

'Well, Father, it's just that it all sounds a bit remote.'

'Remote? In what way?'

Benjamin was silent a moment before replying. 'Remember what you were telling me about those worker-priests in France? . . .'

'Ah, but I never told you the sequel. The experiment was a failure—a terrible failure.' Goddard wiped the corners of his mouth. Then he took a cigarette from the small gold box on the table. Benjamin tried not to register too much amusement. God smoking!—in front of him? What a tale to carry to the fag-end lillies behind the garden shed.

'Was it?' he said, still fascinated by the image of the man of stone puffing cheerily on an untipped cigarette, the lip end hardly moist at all.

'Indeed, yes. Many priests left their order to get married. Some even joined the Communist Party. You must never believe that Our Holy Mother Church is afraid of concerning herself with social issues but two thousand years of experience has taught her to exercise prudence.'

'But Father, don't you think that it is possible to be a Socialist and a good Catholic at the same time?'

'Certainly not. The Communist regimes of Eastern Europe and the Soviet Union are the most tragically immoral systems man has devised. Their repression of the Faith and their callous disregard for human rights is the triumph of atheism and a terrifying warning of the dangers—'

'But Father, in History class Father Piers was very careful to stress the ideological distinction between socialism and communism. He said it's far too complex a subject. Besides, from the perspective of, say, the Third World countries, Socialism and true Christianity are great allies in the fight against repression. If I were to become a Jesuit, that is what I would want to be a part of.'

Goddard did not particularly agree with the sentiment but enjoyed Benji's impassioned speech. He looked at him hard. Then his gaze softened.

'Your idealism is refreshing, my son, if somewhat misguided. But no doubt first-hand experience will overcome that. Then you will see your obligations in their true perspective. Rampant idealism will be disciplined to more objective acts of service.' With a cobra's wink Goddard changed the subject.

'You have a new friend, I hear.'

'Just somebody I met, and we get on.'

'Do you want to tell me about him,' said Goddard, stubbing out the cigarette.

'Not much to tell, Father. He's just a bloke who's been camping out in the woods.' Benjamin tried to stay as casual as possible.

'Hmm. What is his special attraction for you—apart from being a thief? It was he who broke into the school, was it not?'

'No Father.'

Goddard eyed Benjamin, who stared back with unfaltering innocence.

'His name is Blakey ... well, Charlie. He's interesting and, well, different, I suppose.'

'Go on.'

'Well, he's done a lot of things ...'

'Such as?'

'Things I should like to do. He's ... well, he's free.'

Goddard laughed, 'Free? Free? Oh Benjamin, Benjamin ... freedom ...' He got up and walked to the bay window, turned abruptly, adjusted his sash, then said, very dryly 'Freedom, my son, is the banner the unscrupulous will always choose to march under.'

'Yes Father.' Benjamin made to rise from his chair, but Goddard advanced, forcing him back to his seat by the suddenness of his movement.

'But he tells good stories. He makes me laugh.'

'I'm sorry to do this to you Stanfield, but I must make you promise not to see him again.'

'But I think he's about the best friend I've ever had.'

'What nonsense,' said Goddard kindly, 'look at it clearly, you hardly know him. You must try and find your friends within the school.'

'But Father, he's only here for a few more days, I'll only be able—'

'That's enough,' rasped the priest, sweeping into the main room. 'Promise me you won't see him again.'

Benji was silent. He stared at the tea-table, then into the garden, then out to Basket Wood. Something caught his eye, which brought him out of his chair. From the direction of the river, a flock of birds burst up from the trees, wheeling frenetically in the morning haze, then settled back some distance from where they had arisen. Goddard moved closer to Benjamin.

'I'm waiting, Stanfield. Benjamin, I have great hopes for you. *Please* don't let me down. Promise!'

Benjamin muttered, 'All right Father, I promise,' but his attention was on the strange disturbance in the wood. Goddard beamed his appreciation; he even patted him gently on the head.

Benjamin's face flushed with mutiny. Without looking at the priest, he thanked him for the tea and left through the masters' garden. Goddard watched him disappear down the avenue of shrubbery and turn sharply out of sight back towards the school.

Goddard looked out across the fields to the wood, and smiled to himself. He was immensely pleased about something.

Benjamin did not head straight for the woods. That would have been predictable and he had learned that predictability is a slovenly ally easily gauged by his enemies. Instead he headed for the prefects' room in search of the God Squad. He swiftly established his sovereignty with tales of God's morning tea-party, smoking and all, but kept to himself the news of Goddard's elevation to the principal's seat. He knew more points were to be scored by receiving the news later as if he had known it for ages but as the new head's confidant, had been bound to secrecy. The boys welcomed him, glad that he had apparently seen the error of his ways and bowed to their corporate will. Benjamin challenged Cawley to a tennis match that afternoon and invited all to attend. The challenge was accepted. Manning agreed to be umpire. Arthur announced that he would compere. Benjamin graciously beamed his acceptance of these arrangements.

The bells for lunch rang through the school and the comrades repaired to the dining room in good faith, glad that the would-be prodigal had returned.

Blakey was still half asleep when the panda-car rolled

across the leafy entrance to the Wood King's domain. He was dozing in the hammock, still in the fortune-teller jacket. Constable Paynter walked across the clearing to the bike.

Sergeant Blount approached Blakey who, remaining in the hammock greeted his unexpected visitors with a sovereign affability.

'Afternoon, Comrade. Welcome to the Deep Woods. Nice day, isn't it?'

Blount stood at the end of the hammock, his face within inches of Blakey's bare feet. He raised his eyebrows. 'All right, beautiful, get your rags together and make tracks.'

'But my clothes are wet, sir. It's washing day in the forest.'

'Real joker,' Blount quipped to his colleague. 'They'll dry quick enough once they're on you.'

Blakey remained where he was, buttoning the jacket across his bare torso. 'Who told you I was here?'

'Little birdie.'

'This your bike?' called Paynter across the clearing.

'That's right, sir. Got it in one. He'll be a Sergeant before long. Look out, mate, he'll have your job.'

Blount ignored him. He walked round the camp, lit a cigarette and looked idly into the rucksack that lay by the ashes of last night's fire as Blakey got out of his hammock and pulled on his jeans.

'What is your errand, comrade?'

'I'm not your comrade, shit-face,' said the policeman, with a mirthless chuckle.

'Listen friend, this wood isn't private. It belongs to the People.'

'It belongs to the Forestry Commission—didn't you see the notices?'

'I canna read.'

'Clean the shit out of your eyes.'

Paynter had by now dragged all of Blakey's belongings from beneath the tree and was systematically searching them for drugs. Blount picked up the guitar.

'You play this? The old guitar?' Blakey became nervous of the outsize copper's big hands on his guitar.

'Want me to sing along—soothe the savage beast?'

'Comedian, too,' Blount twanged the strings, ' "When I'm cleaning windows." You know curly, you should go to London.

86

You might earn a fortune. Then you wouldn't have to go nicking food from schools, would you?'

'What are you on about? Look, lay off that, will you? You might break one of the strings.'

Paynter finished his search and came over to Blount, who was strumming even more vigorously at Blakey's earnest request to stop. He began to sing in a ludicrous Scots accent. Paynter grinned.

'Bastards,' muttered Blakey.

Blount stopped and stared at him. 'What did you say?'

Blakey turned to Paynter. 'I'll thank that fat slob to give me my guitar.'

'Sergeant, will you give him his instrument?'

Blount swung the guitar to smash it full across Blakey's face. As he staggered from the blow, the constable leaped expertly behind him, hauled his arms above his head and pulled the celestial jacket over the bloody face, to allow his colleague to hit the defenceless man three rapid blows in the stomach.

Blakey fell to the ground, gasping for air. Paynter kicked him viciously in the ribs. With a painful shudder he fell silent.

Blount bent to examine his handiwork. 'He'll live.' He shouted at the unconscious face, 'Move on, sir, you're trespassing, breaking and entering, in possession of dangerous drugs, corrupting minors—but we are pressing no charges.' They left the clearing and returned to their car. Blakey lay still and silent as the rooks returned to inspect the camp.

Benjamin walked off the tennis court without shaking Cawley's hand. He had thrashed him mercilessly and wanted the assembled Houses to know that it was more than just a sporting tournament. He handed the racquet to Sackville and moved over to his tracksuit lying on the terraced lawn. Arthur hobbled over to him.

'Well played, Benji. You'll beat Bjorg next. You were so good. Cawley didn't know what hit him. Benji, believe me, it wasn't me who wanted to tell God, we had a vote and Dowd volunteered.'

'It doesn't matter, Arthur, Goddard knew already.'

'Is he still in the woods?'

'I don't know. I don't really care.'

'Listen, Benji, I want to make this up to you so we can still be friends. If you want to go out tonight, I'll cover for you. I can put pillows under your bedclothes and Goddard'll think you're in there, dead to the world. He won't find out, I'll see to that! And I've got a spare pair of shoes as well. I'll put them under your bed. What do you say?'

'I think we've just about covered all this, haven't we, Arthur?'

'Then you'd like me to do it for you?'

'Take a pew, Arthur.'

Arthur sat on the sloping terrace with great difficulty. Despite his handicap, he was quite agile on his feet, but manoeuvring into and out of sitting positions was rather awkward. When he was finally settled, Benjamin leant over and whispered in his ear.

'You're a tiresome little wanker, Arthur.' Then he sprang up and darted away towards the school. Arthur tried to follow but slipped on the sloping turf.

By late afternoon the sky had become quite overcast. A storm rumbled impatiently in the south-west and the clouds seemed heavy with rain. Benjamin passed most of the day in full view, going about the school, even offering to relieve for an hour one of the prefects supervising a junior class. Just before five, in the evil green afternoon, he walked to the gatehouse, pretending to visit the Gatekeeper, but doubled back round the school until he felt it was safe to scale the stone wall into the woodland estate.

He saw Blakey crawling slowly across the clearing, each movement causing him to moan. Bloodied, leafy, he looked like some mythical beast, part man, part dragon. The sight was deeply, morbidly fascinating to Benji as he ran to him, through the trees.

'Blakey, Blakey! Who has done this to you?'

No response.

'Blakey! Can you hear me?' No response. He half-lifted him and dragged him to the camouflaged bower and covered him with a dirty pale-blue blanket. Tears filling his eyes, he bent and gently kissed the silent face. He left him, to gather up the belongings scattered about the clearing, dumping them in a

heap beside the bike. Blakey stirred. Benji shuffled to his side.
'Charlie! Charlie, it's me, Benji.' The tears poured down
his face. Blakey just looked at him and said nothing.

Benjamin returned to the school the way he had come,
wondering all the way what he should do. For many reasons
he decided to tell no one of Blakey's condition, but to return
that night and minister to him himself.

The staff meeting finished about six, and a Benediction for
the staff was announced, to take place in the chapel. All were
welcome to attend. Before the final recessional, Goddard
mounted the pulpit and read an extract from St Matthew's
Gospel.

'An enemy has done this. Then they said, "Shall we pull
out the weeds?" And he answered, "No, for you may easily
pull out the good wheat at the same time. They shall grow together until the harvesting and at that time the reapers shall
gather the weeds first, and they shall be tied in bundles for
burning. But the good wheat I shall take into my barn." '

It was a most curious choice for the reading. Goddard
aimed almost all his words at Benjamin, who sat alone, ashen-
faced, in a pew at the back of the chapel.

'Satan is, of course, the enemy, and the weeds are sinners.
No, worse than that. To a certain extent we are all sinners.
But there are those whose lives are given over to evil; they
are the weeds and they look remarkably like wheat. Try to get
rid of them while they are still growing, and there is a real
danger of pulling out the wheat with them.' Goddard's eyes
were fixed on Benjamin. 'Only when a good weed has sprouted
does it show itself for what it is—something dangerous, something evil, something planted by the enemy. And it shall be
gathered up, and cast into the fire, and burned.'

A couple of the priests and lay teachers chanced the occasional sideways glance at this odd aria, but Goddard's eyes
did not leave Benjamin, who just sat and stared coldly at the
altar, and at the fitful flashes of lightning that splashed life
into the stained-glass triptych above it. Goddard emerged from
his reverie and dismissed his congregation. Father Henry
chuckled to himself as he played the inappropriately gentle

recessional hymn—raging evangelical hallelujahs would have been more appropriate to the performance he had just heard from below.

Benjamin decided to take up Arthur's offer of help. Grabbing him after tea, he made no apology for his behaviour that afternoon but assured him that it had been necessary if he were ever to go to the woods again. Arthur seemed convinced, especially after being treated to a lurid description of Blakey's wretched condition, but, as usual, asked too many questions —so many, in fact, that Benjamin lost his temper and gave up the whole idea. Arthur stumbled down the top corridor at his heels, pleasing to be readmitted to his confidence. Benjamin feigned reluctance, Arthur crawled even more, and the plot was finally laid.

An hour after lights out Benjamin would go to the wood while Arthur remained awake to cover for him if necessary. Benjamin accepted the spare pair of shoes, but suggested that Arthur sleep in *his* bed and fill his own with pillows. This idea did not appeal in the slightest—Arthur feared that if Goddard were to discover the deception he would be merciless with him and comparatively gentle with Benji.

Benjamin took a small first-aid kit from the gym; he tried to persuade Fat Mary to allow him some of the whisky stored in the kitchen, but she refused, so he stole some communion wine instead. All went smoothly, and at the appointed hour he crept across the fields into the wood. Though the night remained windy and overcast, the storm had passed without rain.

When he arrived at the camp, Blakey was awake, still propped against the bike, shrouded in the blanket and shakily smoking a cigarette.

'What do you want?'

'I brought some ointment for the cuts. I'll get some water from the river. There's some grog here.'

Blakey took the bottle and held it up. Benji unscrewed the top. The injured man drank, but each swallow caused him pain. He said nothing more. Benji took a small metal cup from the first-aid kit and disappeared towards the river. He was soon back.

'I'm sorry for what happened, I really am. God made me

promise not to come here again.'

'What the fuck are you doing here then? Go on, fuck off, I can look after myself. Go.'

'Who hurt you?'

Blakey laughed.

'You.'

Benji did not accept that remark. He took out a torch and propped it on the ground, then soaked a wad of cotton wool in the water he had brought. Blakey continued smoking as Benji began washing away the dirt and congealed blood. Blakey stared straight ahead, unmoving and silent. Benjamin now put some ointment on his fingers and carefully, caressingly, smoothed it into the wounds. Blakey grabbed him by the hair and he recoiled with shock. 'The Good Samaritan act doesn't mean a thing—understand?' Benjamin attempted to continue his ministrations. Blakey pushed him violently away.

'What's your fantasy, cattle-tick? Love thine enemy? I should have realised you were dangerous. Well, I can see that now—why, your precious Father sent the pigs in to butcher me. Not for the stealing, but because he thought I was after a piece of you. Well before I leave here I'm going to do a real razor-job on him.' He looked down at himself, laughed, then looked at Benjamin. 'Okay. You want to help me?'

'Of course I do. That's why I came, that's why I broke my promise, I'd do anything for you.'

'Pack everything up. Pack the bike ready to leave.'

Benjamin complied, while Blakey attempted to dress himself. His inability to do anything properly only increased his frustration. Benjamin finished the packing easily. He tore down the canopy, neatly rolled it with the sleeping bag and tied the bundle to the pillion of the bike. Then he helped Blakey dress, a wildness and desperation in his eyes.

'You're not leaving tonight, you can't leave now. Blakey, please, you'll never manage, you're too awkward, you'll crash and kill yourself.'

'Good. That's what I want.'

'Then take me with you, I've got no one to turn to, to talk to. I want to be with you, I want to be with you. They'll drive me crazy at that place, I'm alone without you, I'm alone.'

'It's too late. We're all damned from the moment we're born. You're all in it together, pigs, teachers, religions—all

91

the little Gods of the world, all part of one big conspiracy. Take a look at yourself in the mirror. You're one of them. Look at your face. Look at your hands. One of them ... You're a weak, spoilt brat ... I thought we were friends, here, I held you here—' He grabbed Benji's hand and placed it on his heart. 'I felt you in here. But now I hate you more than anything else in the world.'

'Don't say that!' cried Benji through his tears. Please ...'

'Look, just fuck off will you,' Blakey yelled suddenly, thrusting Benji violently away.

Benjamin's fury burst into the night like the screech of an owl and he fled out into the clearing. Blakey's laughter followed him, a choking, empty mock, like the crackle of dry thorns. Benji fell silent. The first-aid bag was thrown out at him, then the torch. Then they stood, eyes full of hate, looking at each other across the clearing, hearts hungry for each other's pain. Benji spoke, his voice suffused with rage. 'I'll get you all—you, Goddard, anyone.'

Blakey spat onto the ground and turned away.

Benjamin put the broken chain inside his pocket. Then stooped and found a large heavy stone and hurled it with all his might into the darkness before him.

He had run all the way back to the school, but the morning was running faster, and it was quite light when he arrived at the foot of the stairs to his dormitory. In the yellow-grey light, at the head of the stairs, stood Goddard.

Benjamin stopped.

They faced each other in battle for the first time, not master and pupil, not even Father and My Son, but two very violent hearts. He did not speak as he began the deliberate ascent towards Goddard. On the first step he damned and cursed his betrayer—most likely Arthur, unable to resist telling one of the others, who had told another, and so on till Goddard was told. Then he cursed Goddard for Blakey's beating. It was obvious now that while God was entertaining in the principal's room that morning, the police had been in Basket Wood doing his dirty work. He was within a few steps of the priest, and at the height of a cold rage, and had lessened somewhat his tactical disadvantage.

'It has been reported to me that you spent this past night

in the company of that boy Charlie. Is this true?'

'Yes Father.' He took one step up closer.

'In other words, you deliberately disobeyed my directive that you were not to associate with him.'

'Yes. I did. Who sneaked?' Benjamin seethed, mounting closer.

'Never mind. He has been dealt with.' Goddard's voice was raised, ever so slightly—enough to reverberate in the hollow halls. He loathed creeps and sneaks worse than the miscreants they betrayed, sometimes punishing them more severely. In this case, where the victim was his beloved Stanfield, there was no doubt a detention sleeping with the informant now.

'You, Stanfield, are a disgrace to the school and a reproach to my teaching. You submit to every temptation without the vestige of a struggle, and you court violence and evil as if they were your bedfellows.'

'I'm sorry Father.'

'No, Benji, you are not sorry. There is not a speck of contrition in your eyes. You are only sorry you have been found out. You will play no sports here again until further notice, and you will not attend the break-up picnic tomorrow. You will get down on your hands and knees and clean these stairs and corridors. If that is finished before the end of the day, present yourself to Father Pollard and dig weeds out of the gardens.'

Benjamin attempted to answer.

'I will not hear another word. I am most deeply displeased with you. Now go, before the school wakes up and makes my shame even more public.' He did not move as Benjamin passed by.

Suddenly the boy turned and rushed at him. He grasped his arm. If Goddard had not been a sturdy man, the shock would have sent him hurtling down the stairs. But Benjamin did not want that at all. He had something more startling prepared.

'Father, Father, I want to talk to you about this. It's very important you hear me. You see, I need your help more than ever now, more than anything else in my life. Because something terrible has happened to me.'

Goddard unfastened the grip. 'Well, what do you want of me?'

'Will you hear my confession, now?'

'You know I cannot do that.'

'But you must hear me,' cried Benjamin, in a desperate and pleading voice.

'As your form master and the principal of the school, I am unable to do so. It could put us in a most invidious position having regard to my duty to punish and reward. Listen, my son, you're in enough trouble as it is. If you wish to confess, go to one of the chaplains before dawn. Father Mathews is saying the early mass. I'm sure he will hear you willingly.'

'I couldn't,' shouted Benjamin.

'Why not?'

'Because ... because of what I have to confess. It is for you, or no one. I'd rather die with the sin.'

'Stanfield! Stop these cheap theatricals and go to bed.'

'Please!'

'I tell you, stop this nonsense!' Goddard paced away down the corridor.

Benjamin fell to his knees, in tears. Goddard returned to his apartment, but Benjamin followed him. 'Please, Father! Please hear me!'

Goddard was quite unsettled by this flood of emotion and worried by those great debilitating heaving sighs that accompanied each plea. Stanfield had never shown emotion before. Something must be dangerously wrong.

'Very well. Kneel down there.'

He closed the door, took down the purple stole, kissed it, and sat sideways on the chair, facing away from Benji. The boy blessed himself and began the prescribed confession. 'In the name of the Father and of the Son and of the Holy Ghost Amen. Bless me Father for I have sinned,' he whispered.

'May the Lord lie in your heart and on your lips that you may with truth and humility confess all your sins. In the name of the Father, and of the Son, and the Holy Spirit. Amen.'

'Bless me Father, for I have sinned. It is two weeks since my last confession.' There was a pause.

'Yes, my child.'

'I have committed a grievous sin. Twice, Father.'

'Yes, what kind of sin?'

'Impurity, Father.'

'Impurity, Benjamin? What do you mean?'

'Charlie and I swam naked together in the river.'

'Now be careful Benjamin, swimming naked is not a sin, it is merely indiscreet. Impurity has nothing to do with these matters. Your only sin as far as I can see is disobedience.'

'I understand, Father, but nonetheless I accuse myself of impurity. For these, and all the other sins I cannot remember, I am truly sorry and humbly beg pardon of God, and penance and absolution of you.'

'That is all very well, Benji, but I'm afraid you will have to be more specific.'

Benjamin raised his eyes. Goddard was not looking at him. His hand covered the whole of the side of his face, leaving only the ear exposed. Benjamin bent closer to the ear.

'Well, Father,' he whispered, as softly as he could, 'whoever sneaked on me didn't know anything about me and Charlie, really.'

'Go on. Tell me everything.'

'Charlie and I have known each other carnally. He is my lover.'

Goddard's face fell with a sudden deep-felt anguish. It seemed to lose all shape, all colour.

Benjamin saw none of this—all he saw was the impassive hand and listening ear. But he felt the man's temperature rise as the thorn punctured his heart.

'What kind of thing did he make you do?' intoned that heart, almost struggling to form the words. Benjamin had another thorn prepared.

'He didn't make me, Father. I wanted him to.' Goddard's hand moved from the side of his face and settled across his eyes.

'Did you realise what you were doing is unnatural and wrong?'

'Blakey's very free, Father. He said we should experience everything and judge it for ourselves.'

'Do you agree with that!'

'No Father.'

'I should hope not, my son. This is a very serious matter. You are in mortal sin.'

'I know that Father. But it all happened so suddenly, this need for him. I mean, he is so strong and alive, not like the boys at school. And he knows so much about the world and he's so beautiful.'

'Beautiful,' said Goddard to himself.

'Yes. Like an animal. He is quick like a darting silver fish, proud and hard like a bull, and wild, and then gentle.'

'I realise by these flights of poetic fancy just how far under this lad's influence you have sunk.' Goddard shifted irritably in his seat. Oblivious to the deeper hurt, Benjamin's thirst for revenge was satisfied by this discomfort and irritation. He continued his confession along the same lines.

'Couldn't the whole thing have been something like the ecstasy those mystics had when He expressed His Love?'

'Certainly not!' snapped the priest. 'Don't be stupid. There is a world of difference between revealed spiritual truths and grubby adolescent sexual experimentation.'

'Yes Father. Sorry.'

'Benjamin, are you not ashamed and disgusted that you permitted such abominations to take place, that you should permit your body to be a part of something so wrong, so unnatural? Sex, Benjamin—sex is a God-given instinct that must be cherished carefully until it may be used in accordance with God's Holy Sacrament: marriage. Is that clear?'

'Yes, Father.'

'Are you truly contrite?'

'Yes Father, I am deeply ashamed and disgusted with myself.'

'And so you resolve never to sin like this again, never to see Blakey again?'

'Yes Father, there is no danger of that, I promise you.'

'Benjamin, do not hasten to accuse yourself of what in all probability you have not done. There may have been a certain intimacy between you, even a physical familiarity, but I feel from what you've told me ... well, you are an imaginative boy, and besides, he is older than you, and knows more of the world. I am quite sure he was the moving spirit in this affair.'

Benjamin received this curious, halting lesson with smug delight. 'Thank you, Father.'

'Good, good ...' said Goddard. He was still in a state of shock. 'For your penance you will offer five decades of the Rosary to Our Lady that she might henceforth guide you and intercede for you.' He began the act of contrition. 'Oh my God ...' Benjamin repeated the phrase, then continued the prayer.

'Oh my God I am sorry and beg pardon for all my sins. I detest them because they deserve thy dreadful punishments, because they crucified my loving Saviour.'

Goddard prayed with him. His gaze never left the nails in the polished wood floor. They were all he could see through the slits between his fingers.

'God the Father of mercies, through the death and resurrection of his Son has reconciled the world to Himself and sent the Holy Spirit amongst us to the forgiveness of sins . . .'

Benjamin had not yet risen when Goddard called Sackville to his room. He ordered Dowd and Dyson to be sent to him before breakfast. In the shower room, Dowd received the news with a shrug of his shoulders. 'When I'm dressed,' he said.

But Arthur, who was in the toilet reading the best-seller about the Bermuda Triangle, became rather agitated. The only thing he and Dowd had in common was their involvement in Benji's indiscretions. Dowd had reported Blakey, and Arthur's ineptitude had exposed rather than concealed Benji's absence. Peterson woke Benjamin, so he was out of earshot when the rest of the Squad were startled to hear the whistle and crack of the cane. Most of them couldn't believe their ears, for surely Goddard, was the champion of never daring to resort to brutish measures?

Benjamin returned to the dormitory as they came out of Goddard's apartment, Dowd's face black with rage and humiliation. Poor Arthur could only manage humiliation. No one spoke, for Goddard himself, still brandishing the stick, appeared in the doorway. 'Stanfield,' he bellowed. 'In here now.'

More surprises—God was going to punish the beloved son.

Benjamin walked past the priest into the room. Goddard followed, closing the door behind them. Instantly ears were pressed to the walls, straining to hear the telling cuts. But nothing came. Dowd went to his cubicle and pulled the curtain. Arthur limped out of the dormitory. He could not bear the others to hear his sobbing.

Goddard motioned Benjamin, who was quite shocked at this turn of events, to take a seat. The priest sat behind his desk, placing the cane in front of him. Benjamin's thrill at having

97

unnerved Goddard was tempered with fearful anticipation. He knew he could bear the cane, but felt the punishment would belittle him. He was already steeling himself to the degradation of scrubbing stairs and corridors but this would add injury to insult. He spoke.

'Father, are you going to cane me for what I told you in confessional?'

'How dare you suggest such a thing, Benjamin. I have already told you what your punishment is and you will begin it after breakfast. I cannot punish you for anything you tell me in the confessional. I have caned Dyson for being a party to your escapades and persistently lying to me. I have caned Dowd for his callous and self-interested informing on one of his fellow pupils. He actually had the effrontery to inform me of his reasons for telling on you. They were spiteful. One cannot reason with boys like that.' The bells were ringing for breakfast. 'You must be careful, Benji. I'm sure many people find you an attractive boy, but you must not let yourself be beguiled by these things. They mean nothing in the long run. Remember the poems we were looking at only a few days ago. There is a great truth in them. Perhaps you should commit them to memory—yes, while you are performing the menial tasks today, turn the punishment into something worthwhile by learning the poems.' Goddard got up and took the cane. 'Come on, off you go to breakfast.'

As they left the room, Arthur clumped in from the toilets. 'Come on, Dyson, why is it you are always hanging about?'

'I wasn't, Father, I was just going—'

'Arthur, you have a rare genius for lurking which virtually elevates peripatetic activity into a fine art. Have you nothing better to do?' Goddard swept out of the dormitory, tapping the cane gently on the skirting of his soutane.

'A fine mess you got me into, Stanfield.'

'I'm sorry, Arthur. I'm in trouble as well.'

'Maybe, but I notice he didn't touch you.'

'No, he's got worse lined up. I can't go on the picnic this afternoon. I've got to spend the day scrubbing floors, digging the bloody garden.'

'That's really nothing. God would forgive you anything.'

Benjamin smiled to himself as Arthur headed towards

breakfast. He was feeling quite pleased with himself. He had killed two birds with one stone. But still he was not satisfied.

He arrived late for breakfast, just managing to charm tea and toast from the cook. Then he joined Cawley and the others in the courtyard outside. 'All the science results will be given this morning.' He feigned interest and immediately changed the subject to the strange events of the morning.

'I told him Charlie was my lover. I said I had been impure, that I had known him carnally dozens of times.' Most of them couldn't quite believe what they were hearing.

'What did he say to that?'

'What can he say? He choked to hell, but he can't say anything.'

'Come off it, Benjamin, you didn't really.'

'I did. I told him that sex with Blakey was everything I ever wanted. He is strong and warm and animal ...'

'You told him all this in confession?' gulped Hardy.

'Of course. You're supposed to put things in your own words, aren't you? Anyway, God got fearfully cut up, which was the object of the exercise.'

'Why did you do it?' Sackville was not at all impressed.

'I have my reasons.'

Boys began moving off, as class was about to begin.

The Picnic Tea at Sommerbury began around two-thirty. The weather was hot and humid. Most of the boys wore their whtie sports coats with the red sacred heart emblazoned on the breast pockets, and the priests, instead of their soutanes, dressed casually in white open-neck shirts with tiny gold crosses sparkling on their collars. It was quite a spectacle: the long trestle tables were covered with sheets and piled with cakes and sandwiches and an inordinate amount of nausea-inducing goodies.

Meanwhile Goddard checked on Benjamin, who was down on his hands and knees, scrubbing the corridors. Goddard, immaculate in a white soutane, passed him without speaking, but smiled to see his corrected son bending to his task.

Benjamin had just finished washing one large section of stairs when Father Roberts and a large group of younger boys laden with cricket equipment trooped down the stairs, leaving a broad trail of muddy footprints. He ignored their jeers and laughter and painstakingly erased their footwork.

'Cor luv a duck! If it ain't old Mrs Mopp!' Dowd mocked from the top of the stairs. 'Hard on the knees, is it me old darlin'?'

'Get stuffed, Dowd.'

Dowd slid his foot towards the bucket. It lurched, and clattered down the stairs. Water poured everywhere. He walked down past the kneeling boy.

'Sorry Benji. You'll have to start again.'

Benji was about to hurl the scrubbing brush at his tormentor when the Brigadier appeared.

'What do you think you're doing, fellow?'

'Nothing sir, it wasn't my fault.'

'It's never your fault, fellow. Get on with your work or I'll have you scrubbing out the latrines as well.'

Dowd greeted the irate teacher. 'Good afternoon, sir. Will you be joining us at the picnic?'

They passed out into the courtyard.

Benji put his hands in his pockets. Blakey's gold chain caught his attention. He picked up the bucket and brush and headed outside towards the gardens.

When tea was finished, the boys and priests broke into smaller groups to enjoy various activities. Goddard and Moore wandered over to the verge of the wood where Father Gladstone and some of the older boys were playing around a rope contraption erected by the cadets. Strains of the school orchestra, playing on the upper lawns, gave the hot afternoon a raucous carnival atmosphere.

'The picnic is going splendidly this year, Moore.'

'Yes. It's a pity Father Rivers is not well enough to join us.'

Goddard was in quite a good humour, considering the fury in which he had begun the day. He pointed out the cricket match to Father Moore. Father Piers was being bowled at by a wild, ginger-haired fourth-former.

'I do enjoy seeing them at play in this atmosphere. Young people have a tremendous ability to enjoy—a quality only too easily lost in this world.

> ' "Oh dearest, dearest boy, my heart
> For better love would seldom yearn
> Could I but teach the hundredth part
> Of what from them I learn."

You remember Wordsworth, Father Moore?'

'Yes indeed, Father. Profoundly wistful lines—you're delivery does them great service. But surely we should all be on our guard against the immoderate worship of youth so fashionable today?'

'Oh Michael, don't be so stuffy. I think we should be most on our guard against replacing wonder with sophistry. After all, that's how faith eventually gets locked out.'

Moore indicated the group of God Squad regulars clustered around the rope and Father Gladstone. 'Little chance of sophistication with that lot!'

'Hello Father,' Gladstone shouted. 'There is a debate going on here about some aerial adventures I've suggested.'

'Isn't it a bit soon after tea for this sort of strenuous physical activity, Father? I don't think we should be encouraged to do anything too high above the ground on a full stomach.'

Goddard laughed. 'Do you the world of good, Manning. You're getting quite chubby. Besides, I've heard that climbing arranges the food in the stomach and altitude aids the digestion tremendously.'

'If it speeds the whole process up that quickly, isn't it dangerous to stand so close under the rope?' gulped Cawley.

'You can hold the rope, Terry, and we'll find out,' riposted Gladstone. Dowd, quite physically adept, scampered up the rope and displayed his gymnastic skills. The boys generously applauded his graceful solo flight. 'All right, Dowd, down you come.' He leaped from the rope and landed with a circus-style flourish. Goddard walked forward and put his hand on his shoulder.

'Splendid, Dowd, very graceful. Your hard work in the gym has paid off. Well done.'

Gladstone turned to Arthur. 'Come on, your turn next.'

'No Father, please, someone else, I'm not any good at those kind of things.'

Gladstone persisted, encouraged by Goddard. Neither seemed aware of the devastating cruelty of the situation. The boys urged Arthur on. He had seen how warmly Goddard had applauded Dowd's efforts, so despite his better judgement, he decided to make an attempt. Surely that was all this facile game required.

'Come, I'll help you,' said Goddard. 'There, you're not going to fall, don't even think about it. Now, how's that?'

Arthur enjoyed the priest's attention. Dowd hurried to assist. 'But my leg, Father.'

'Don't Arthur,' encouraged Goddard.

'Take heart, Arthur. If you fall there's only one left to break,' cracked Manning, hoping for a big laugh.

'That's enough, Manning.'

Arthur made tentative progress—childhood years spent in a wheelchair had made his shoulders and upper body quite strong. He managed to heave himself up the rope.

'That's it, Arthur.'

'Yes, well done, my son.'

Arthur reached the top. 'Father, Father, I think I'm going to fall.'

'You can't fall, Arthur, if you're holding the rope.'

'Give him a turn,' said Goddard and Dowd swung the rope as if the boy were an acrobat. As at a public execution, the primary expression was one of silent awe. One or two of the crass hearts were amused; one or two of the finer souls disgusted. Goddard remained affable.

'Stop, please! I want to come down! Father, stop them!'

'Oh Arthur,' said Goddard tetchily. 'Stop whining. Don't spoil things.'

Arthur screamed. 'Please, Father. I'm frightened. I've had enough.' He let go of the rope with one hand and reached out to Goddard. 'Father, Father, help me!'

'For God's sake, Arthur, grip the rope!' shouted Father Gladstone. 'Use both hands, Arthur, ease yourself down. You're only making it worse for yourself.'

Dowd stopped the rope taut. Arthur hung inert and terrified.

'Come on down then,' said Father Moore, kindly. Slowly and shamefully, Arthur descended. He had wanted to please God with his daring and so earn an affectionate gesture, after the caning. Now this squealing ineptitude made him all the more pathetic in Goddard's eyes.

'Virtutus omnis impedimentum est tima, as Publius Syrus

has it. Fear, my child, is a hindrance to all virtue.' Goddard looked contemptuously at him. Arthur let go the rope and dropped to the ground. 'Pick him up, someone.' Dowd frowned, but obeyed.

The afternoon continued without fuss, until the various groups began drifting back to the school. A violent evening storm was charging across from the west, clouds dark and heavy with rain. Goddard was playing blind man's bluff with a group of very young boys when the first spits from Heaven began.

'Come on all of you, we'll go to the chapel and make a visit. Thanking God for this lovely day. Besides, if we stay out, we'll get drenched.'

The rain hurtled down. Hailstones clattered onto the courtyard and vanished. Daylight melted away to the vague patches of afternoon sky the advancing clouds had not reached. Lightning sliced the overheated air inside the chapel. Goddard and the boys stood before the altar. En masse, they genuflected. He blessed them and they dispersed.

When they'd gone he began his own prayer.

'Oh glorious John the Baptist de la Salle, protector of children and young folk, be thou from the height of Heaven my patron and my guide. Help me, that I may be preserved from every stain of error and corruption, so I might guide these young people to the feet of the divine Master.' He dropped to his knees and clasped his hands tightly, resting his head on the knotted thumbs. 'St John Bosco, be thou my example in this precious dealing with young souls ...'

Unseen, Benjamin entered the chapel, soaked with rain, his hands and clothes covered with moist red mud.

'Oh give me strength,' continued the priest, 'to devote myself unsparingly to supporting them against the snares and seductions of the Devil, and in keeping them safe from the dangers of this world. Amen.' He rose, genuflected, and moved down the aisle towards the door. He was within a few feet of it when Benjamin, wild and wet like Edgar from King Lear, caught his eye. He stared at the muddy spectacle.

'Benjamin,' said God's voice of ice.

'Father.'

'You gave me your word, a sacred oath in the confessional

that you would never again seek out the company of that creature, yet by your condition I can see that you have been again to the river. Can you explain yourself? Do you hear me? Lift up your eyes and look straight at me when I am speaking to you. Well? Well! Explain. Come on, I'm waiting.'

'Something came over me. I had to go to him.'

'Lie.'

'I couldn't help it.'

'Lie.'

'I—'

'Lie. Not a word more. I am sick of the sound of your voice. You're a disgrace to the school, to that uniform, to your rank as an altar boy, to your aspirations of priesthood and to your faith. It's all finished, Benji, your future is wasted by the ignominy of your present behaviour. I am deeply shocked and ashamed. I fear for you. You are worth nothing to me any more.'

Benjamin burst into uncontrolled sobs. He staggered towards the priest and gripped his arm. Goddard violently disengaged the muddy fingers from his white sleeve.

'Please, Father, I must confess to you.'

'No.'

'Father, you can't refuse me. I have too serious a sin on my soul.'

Something in Benjamin's sudden strange calm persuaded the priest that, despite the ever-present hysterics, the boy was in trouble. He sent him to the confessional to prepare himself. Goddard walked back down the aisle and crossed from the sanctuary into the sacristy. Benjamin knelt in the confesional box. He heard Goddard enter the confessor's cubicle and the squeak of the chair as he settled himself.

'Bless me Father for I have sinned. At my last confession I told you about the carnal knowledge and although I swore never to see Charlie again, the attachment was too strong.'

'I know all this. You have been punished for it.'

Benjamin lowered his voice and pressed his face to the grille. 'This afternoon—'

'Benjamin, don't lean in like that. It distorts your voice. Kneel up straight and speak quietly and distinctly.'

There was a pause, a loud sniffle, and he went on. Goddard sat staring at the portrait of the Madonna Dolorosa on the wall of the cubicle. In one corner, damp had eaten its way to the heart with its seven blades.

'While you were at the picnic I defied you because I was angry with you. I was working in the garden as you told me. I had to dump the weeds near the wood. Well, there was so much going on that I was able to slip into the wood unnoticed and I went looking for Charlie. I found him. He had recovered from his beating by the police and was preparing to leave. I couldn't bear the thought of him going. After what we'd been through, I wanted him to stay. I couldn't bear the thought of him having a good time with other boys. He was like my brother. No, better than my brother, he was a lover. He was even a father. So—I started thinking of ways of keeping him near me. There was only one way that worked.'

'Benjamin, what do you mean?'

'I was possessed, Father, I must have been. I cannot remember exactly what I was feeling. We walked around through the woods, it was very hot before the storm. We took off our clothes. We had sex. Then he said. "I'm off", just like that. I said, "Don't go, you mustn't go." He just laughed at me. So I got furious. I picked up this rock and . . .'

Goddard leaned forward in his chair. 'Yes? And . . .'

'I hit him on the head with it. Killed him instantly. It smashed open his temple.' Goddard gurgled in disbelief.

'You murdered him?'

'Yes. Well, I didn't know what was happening, I couldn't help myself. Everything became misty, red and black. I couldn't help myself. Suddenly, he was lying there on the grass . . . blood . . . not much.' His voice dissolved to whispering cries, to silence. Then, 'Oh help me, Father, I can't bear it, help me!'

For a moment Goddard sat, pale and confused. He tried to speak, but at first words failed him. 'I will try and help you.'

'Oh I knew I could count on you Father.'

'Firstly, you must keep in the forefront of your mind that God will never desert a wholly repentant sinner, no matter what he has done. The only immediate comfort I can give is that it's plain from your description of this most horrible crime, that passion may have robbed you of the use of free will at the time of its commission.'

'I'd give anything for Charlie to be alive . . .' The sentence dissolved into sobbing.

'Yes, I believe that. You have, alas, realised too late that ultimately you can govern nothing in this world but your own soul.'

There was an interminable silence between them. Finally, Goddard spoke again. 'Benjamin, because of the gravity of this confession, I need time to consider it before I absolve you. Go into the sacristy where you can be alone. Say the Rosary, the full sorrowful mysteries, contemplate each one seriously and ask the Holy Spirit for guidance.'

Goddard sat shocked. He heard Benjamin enter the sacristy. He left the confessional and closed the door. After a while, when he had considered his course of action, he followed, Benjamin was praying as instructed. Goddard stood near him. Finally he said, 'Benji. Because of the seriousness of the sin, I need . . .'

'Father you have my permission to discuss it with me outside the confessional. If that is what you need . . . I'll do anything for your help.'

'Yes of course. But let us say this is a continuation of your confession. It is irregular, but the gravity of your . . . predicament warrants it. Rest assured, though, that the confidence of the sacrament remains. You must always feel safe confiding your deepest secrets to God.'

'I do Father. I trust you.'

'That is not what I meant.'

'And God too,' finished Benjamin. The tears and mud on his face had long since dried.

'The thought has occurred to me that often when we wish something to happen we dream it, and the dream is so vivid we think it actually happened to us.'

'You think I dreamed I killed Charlie?'

'Yes . . . yes.'

'No Father, it was no dream,' said Benji, standing up, 'I killed him.' Goddard motioned him to kneel again, agitated but still unconvinced.

'Is it possible that in error you may have exaggerated what you did to Charlie? You may have struck him but not really killed him.'

Benjamin became very serious. There was no pleading in his

voice. 'Father, believe me, you are wrong. I didn't dream it and I didn't exaggerate. I know what I'm doing. Go and see yourself. I had to bury the body.'

Goddard reeled at the mention of a body. For the first time he began to believe that Benji had actually committed murder. 'Oh my God! A body. Of course. Tell me, where is the grave?'

'It's very near, Father. In Basket Wood there is a disused well, quite near to the river. A shallow ditch connects this well to the main stream. Blakey's body is there, in the ditch, under the fallen elm.'

'I know where the elm is. I'll find it. I'll go there now. You will wait here for my return. 'He reached into a cabinet. From it he took the emergency kit which contained the necessary articles to administer Extreme Unction on the corpse. He was taking no chances, hoping still that Benji was exaggerating but preparing for the worst. He hurried out of the chapel into the windy night.

Behind him, Benji sat on for a few moments, smiling fearfully. Then he rose abruptly and left the chapel.

With his face set grimly against the whirling darkness, Goddard crossed the school grounds, and took a spade from the gardener's shed. Thus armed, he set course for the woods, climbing higher and higher, oblivious of the wind that sucked at his soutane, the lightning that flash-bulbed the whipping branches, the lancing rain that fragmented the stares of the cringing night animals.

Not pausing for an instant, he waded across the swollen river and found the disused well and fallen elm all too quickly.

He bent down. There, beneath the stricken tree, was a mound of freshly tumbled earth. He started back at the sight, then, with a great effort, he pulled himself together and started to dig with the spade, slowly at first, then more and more feverishly, stopping every so often to make sure he was unobserved.

Suddenly a final spadeful of earth uncovered the grave's occupant—a wooden scarecrow figure with a hideous pumpkin face. Round its neck was Blakey's gold cross and chain.

From the nearby darkness came a soft, half-suppressed giggle.

'Who's there?' cried Goddard. 'Stanfield? ... Is that you

Stanfield? . . . Come out I say.'

The priest stood, turning his head from side to side, peering into the windy darkness. Then suddenly furious, he drove his spade through the pumpkin's grinning face and stumbled from the wood.

Forty feet away, behind the trunk of a huge Chestnut tree, crouched Benjamin, Arthur, and a few members of the God Squad. Only Benjamin was deliriously happy.

'Did you see his face? Wasn't it amazing when he got to the pumpkin,' he crowed. 'He was absolutely livid.'

'You've gone too far this time,' said Hardy. 'It was a rotten trick.'

'I don't think it was all that rotten,' said Arthur.

'What,' said Cawley, 'telling him a lie in confession? It's blasphemy.'

'Blasphemy or not, he can't do anything about it, can he?' Benjamin chortled. 'He's tied by the seal of confession.'

'Come on,' said Dowd. 'Let's get back before he misses us.'

The boys started to run towards the school, ignoring Benjamin's attempts to jolly them into accepting the greatness of the trick. Arthur, bringing up the rear was soon left far behind.

Back in the chapel, the dishevelled priest raged at the cringing figure of Benjamin.

'It's blasphemy on a scale I've never encountered in thirty years as a teacher and priest,' he roared. 'Do you know what you have done? You have had the effrontery to kneel down before your priest and abuse the sacrament of confession. You have gone out of your way to make a mockery of the rites and practices of the church, and you have ended up playing a filthy practical joke on God.'

'Not on God, Father, on *you*,' cried Benjamin.

'On God!' The voice sounded round the chapel, like a clap of thunder. 'When you speak to the priest in the confessional, you speak to God! Quite apart from putting your immortal soul in jeopardy of eternal damnation, you have shown quite plainly with this brutal game that you don't care a fig about what any of us have been trying to teach you. In fact you have held our trust in you in total contempt.' He stopped pacing and looked at the boy. 'Unfortunately you have tied my hands. I'm bound by the holy silence of the confessional—otherwise I'd certainly recommend the board to expel you immediately.'

Benjamin suddenly grabbed the priest's arm and buried his face in his sodden sleeve. 'Listen to me, please. Shouldn't you ask yourself why I did it?'

Goddard roughly shook him off. 'Why should I concern myself with your alley-cat motives?'

'I felt you had turned away from me and were deliberately singling me out for punishment.'

'That's hardly true, Benjamin.'

'You have been like a father to me, better ever than my actual father. You're kinder, more understanding. You wanted to be with me. When you were cruel to me, I hated you, I had to get back at you. I had to show you I cared what you were doing to me and that what you thought of me mattered. Forgive me Father or I'll be lost altogether. I'll go mad.'

Once more Goddard allowed his feelings to override his judgement. Suddenly he grunted, almost smiled. 'Well, Stanfield, I will forgive you. You were obviously in a highly disturbed emotional state, and were not the master of your actions.'

'Oh, thank you Father.'

'But please remember in future I am your teacher and spiritual adviser, and, though during term-time it is true to say that I stand in loco parentis to you, I am not your father.'

'Yes Father.'

'You must therefore make the strongest effort to control your emotional response to my authority and see our relationship in its true perspective. That is how you will win my respect and admiration—behaving well, exercising restraint and showing kindness.

Goddard left the chapel, bewildered and utterly exhausted.

Benjamin sat on in the chapel, smiling a cold contemptuous smile. The hissed sibilants dribbled from the corner of the mouth.

'Damn him! Damn him! Damn him! I hope his stinking filthy flesh bubbles in hell for all eternity.' He slapped his open palm on the stone vault beside him, so that the whole chapel rang with the sound.

Part Four

OUT OF THE DEPTHS

Goddard woke late, and stormed through the dormitory in a foul mood, handing out minor detentions for the slightest offence. His most vicious attack he reserved for the hapless Arthur. If anyone courted trouble, it was he. Goddard caught him in the shower room, combing his hair before the mirror, arranging it in the same style as Benjamin Stanfield—a gesture that might have been designed to infuriate Goddard. Fortunately Arthur's subtle act of adoration went unnoticed.

Instead, exception was taken to Arthur's immoderate use of after-shave. 'Are you using scent, Dyson?'

'No, Father, of course not.'

'Then what is that appalling smell? Come on, boy, give it to me. You know my rules about this sort of thing.' Arthur handed the priest a phallic bottle containing after-shave with the label 'Pagan Man'. Goddard scarcely bothered to conceal his disgust.

'It was a present from my aunt.'

'Oh why do you have to lie, boy, your aunt didn't send it to you.'

'She did!' said Arthur, his teeth clenched in uncharacteristic defiance.

'Does it make you feel more of a man, dousing yourself with cheap perfume?' The defence crumbled. Arthur lowered his head. 'Well does it?' shouted Goddard. 'Come with me.' He stormed out of the showers, into the dormitory and tore open the curtain of Arthur's cubicle. 'Open those drawers.'

'But Father ...' The protest died away as he knelt awkwardly, fumbling with the set of keys on their elaborate chain that he kept on the desk. Goddard looked in the first drawer, then the second. 'Come on, open that bottom one.' Arthur did so, making it look as laborious as possible, hoping for an eleventh hour reprieve, something to divert the priest's attention. None came.

'Empty it.'

'But Father, what have I done?'

'Empty it.'

Resigned, Arthur complied. Under an array of books, at the bottom of the drawer lay a magazine of the Health and Efficiency variety, which featured on its cover a powerfully built young man, completely naked, a stark contrast to the pale awkward boy with an incomplete leg. Arthur did not look up. God was satisfied.

'Destroy it. And you can collect the bottle at the end of term. Bear this in mind, Dyson. In ancient times, true pagan men used to expose any new-born cripples and weaklings on the mountainside. They would not suffer them to live.' He turned on his heel and left.

Word spread like wildfire through the school of the previous night's great hoax.

The hideous decaying body of the scarecrow, now lying in the slight morning sun upon the compost heap, had become a shrine. After breakfast, blazered pilgrims made the obligatory visit to hear the tale retold. Goddard had made no mention of it. His only statement had been that sciences and related results would be returned that morning; English and languages would have to wait another day.

Benjamin's reputation in the school as a whole, had risen, if it were at all possible to rise any further, to a zenith. Rumour is a rolling stone; it gathers so much moss in the retelling that it ceases to resemble its stone beginnings at all. He could not resist embellishing the story, confirming all versions as official and embellishing them still further himself.

'Look here, Father, I said to him. Look here, old man. You may be called God, but you aren't one in fact. If you try and get round the confessional and punish me in some way, I'll have to get my real father to have a word with your superiors and you may very well find yourself giving the sacraments to a few leprous blacks on some snake-infested atoll.'

This fanciful sermon was greeted with much delight by those who knew Benjamin's particular gift for exaggeration. But there were many in the God Squad who disapproved of the blasphemy of the lie in the confessional and gradually his once adoring audience became less responsive.

Benji reacted furiously. 'What are you lot looking at? You're cowards, all of you. You're terrified of being punished. You won't get punished by Goddard or anybody else up there. Know why? Because it's all lies, what we've been told.'

'Then why are you still an altar-boy?' asked Hardy.

'He likes wearing black skirts,' said Dowd. 'Makes him a little God.'

'Yes Benji, you're just another Goddard, mad as he is— maybe that's why you like each other so much.'

Benjamin could say nothing. He reached into his pocket and took out a crumpled cigarette packet and some matches. He stuffed the pack into the chest of the scarecrow and lit it. The cellophane flared briefly, then died. The straw was still damp. The boys began to disperse. Angrily he threw the matches onto the scarecrow and left to attend morning class. By mid-day, the sad dummy was smouldering. By late afternoon, it was eaten away to ashes.

At tea, Benjamin sat alone. Arthur limped up and attempted to make conversation.

'I understand why you did it. I do really. It was, I mean, it was very brave of you. I could hear what God was saying when he came back into the chapel. I admire you for it, honestly. I wouldn't even mind sharing the blame. Even ... well, taking all the blame if you like. I wouldn't mind. I'll go to Goddard and tell him it was my idea.'

Benjamin gave Arthur a sour look. Arthur blinked incessantly behind his glasses.

'Do you know what I wish you were, Arthur?'

'What?'

'A lump of dog-shit on my shoe so I could scrape you off on a stone.' With that he turned and pushed the tiresome friend off the bench. In trying to catch his balance, Arthur pulled his half-filled tea-cup into his lap.

Arthur was going through the awkward procedure of changing his trousers when Benjamin appeared in his cubicle.

'Arthur ...'

'What?' came the sulky reply.

'Well, do you mind if I come in?'

'What do you want?'

'Oh Arthur, please don't be like that.'

'All right,' said Arthur grudgingly.

Benjamin sat on the side of the bed. 'Can I help you ... with your trousers? It must be difficult with the brace.'

'No I can manage. I've done it lots of times.'

'Let me help all the same.'

'I'd rather you didn't.'

Benjamin ignored the refusal and pulled the long grey trousers over Arthur's legs. 'I'm sorry for what I did and said at tea. It was stupid and ...'

'Are you?' snapped Arthur.

'Yes. Truly. It's just that ... well, frankly Arthur, you can be such a wet little prick at times.'

'Thank you very much.'

'No, don't take it like that. I'm trying to make it up to you. I want to help you and I think I know how.' Arthur looked at him, a picture of weary resignation. 'You know you said you'd like to take the blame for the scarecrow?'

'Yes ...' Arthur's reluctance grew.

'Well, why don't you—in confession, like I did. You see, it's simple. When Goddard was shouting at me in there— well, you said you heard him yourself—I could tell he was really terrified of me. If you told him it was all your idea—I know him, the way he thinks, the way he feels—I know he'd respect you for it. There was a moment last night he nearly found it funny. I know how much you like to make people laugh. Well, if you could crack God's face—'

'He didn't sound like he was respecting *you*. I actually thought he might lose control and strangle you.'

'Don't be stupid, Arthur. He was furious because I'd crossed him, but he respected me for standing up to him. Listen,' he pulled Arthur down onto the bed beside him, 'when you break his rules, he doesn't know how to cope. He just blasts away with hot air. Nothing happens. Nothing happened to me and nothing can happen to you—if you do it as part of a formal confession. Besides, it's your chance to get God for all the times he's been beastly to you.'

Arthur reflected on this for a moment. He looked at Benji strangely.

'Decide quickly, Arthur, because tonight is the only night Goddard hears open confession for the lay teachers. If he asks what you are doing there, say it's important you confess to him and not to one of the chaplains. Arthur? Decide. If you bring this off you can have my friendship for life.'

'I will do it, only if you come with me to the chapel.'

'I will come, only if you do it.'

With portentous solemnity, Benjamin spat into his hand. After a moment, Arthur did the same. They clasped their hands tightly together.

There were very few people in the chapel. Mrs Hoskins left the confessional and made her way to the front of the church, where she loudly said her penance at the feet of Our Lady to whom she was eternally grateful.

Fat Mary knelt by the candle tray of St Anthony across the aisle, no doubt asking him to find her some patience with her domineering kitchen supervisor.

Tasker, the gatehouse keeper sat in a pew near the confessional. There was very little light in the chapel—just the candles, the ever-glowing sanctuary light, and the small dim bulb on the confessional to indicate that there was a priest in attendance.

Benji and Arthur sat together, the latter continually rubbing his hands together and inspecting his palms. Tasker got up and went to the confessional.

'What's the matter?' hissed Benjamin.

'Nothing Benji, I'm just a bit jumpy.'

'Be careful, Arthur, don't be nervous once you're inside. There's no point in doing this unless you enjoy it. Any of those nerves and you'll give the game away.'

'I wish I had your nerve, Benji.' The strain had imparted an involuntary jerk to Arthur's hands. Benji could hardly contain himself.

'Take a pill, Arthur.'

'I would if I had any.'

'Oh come on, come on.' Arthur was squirming like a silly puppy with worms.

'Learn to wait, Arthur, you've got to time these things perfectly.'

'Have you seen Blakey lately?' he said, trying to make conversation.

'That shit!' Benji's savagery almost drove Arthur from the chapel, it so astonished him. 'No I haven't seen him lately, and jolly good riddance to him. I'll show them,' he menaced.

'Show them what?' whimpered Arthur, becoming more unnerved by the minute. Benjamin violently grasped his arm. 'Oh Benji, that hurts.'

Benjamin let go. 'Be warned, Arthur, I'll show them.'

'Show them what?'

'You'll see.'

Benjamin got up and moved across to the confessional. 'Now, Arthur. Come on. Well what are you waiting for. Go on.'

Reluctantly Arthur rose and made his way to the confessional. Benji almost had to push him in, for he faltered at the last moment. He hovered near, and could faintly hear the opening address, when a voice beside him said, 'Stanfield!'

'Yes Father Keenan. Good evening. God bless you.'

'What are you doing?'

'Waiting to go to confession, Father.'

'You know better than that, Benjamin, you must wait your turn somewhere else.' And with that he steered the reluctant boy back into the pews.

'I've had defiant thoughts about you, Father. That's why I must confess my sins to you,' mumbled Arthur.

'Speak up, I can't hear you.' Arthur leaned forward till his mouth almost touched the grille.

'I've had defiant thoughts about you, Father.'

'Please keep back from the grille, you only distort the sound,' grunted the priest, clearly far from fresh after absolving a tedious session of venal sins.

'I've had defiant thoughts about you,' said Arthur clearly.

'Defiant thoughts? You must specify their nature.'

'I've taken sides with Stanfield when he defied you and given him the impression I approved of it.'

'Is that it?' said Goddard.

'Yes ... yes,' came Arthur's rather lame reply. There was a pause.

'This is most reprehensible. In your pride you have failed in your duty to submit to the authority of the church and you have stupidly indulged your own weakness. You should find yourself better, more worthy heroes.'

'Yes Father, it's just that I like Benji so much and I want him to like me. I feel so alone sometimes.'

'That is no excuse for sin, is it?'

'No Father.'

In the distance, the organ began to play a processional hymn. Father Keenan was saying an evening mass. Benji, lounging impatiently in his pew, rose and looked about him, then swiftly approached the confessional.

Goddard continued: 'I understand, my child. Adolescence is a stormy time for a boy. You are leaving the serenity and security of childhood and will from time to time feel unwanted and inadequate.'

'Yes Father,' came the thankful reply.

'You will do a penance of twenty-five Hail Marys and attend one Mass. In fact, a mass has just begun. Go now. May the Almighty and merciful God grant thee pardon, absolution and remission of thy sins, Amen.' After a short prayer on his own behalf, Goddard was about to rise and take off the stole when he heard a movement in the box. 'I am sorry, this session has now finished. I can't hear you now.'

'Please Father, it won't take long and I can't go to communion with a stain on my soul.'

'Benjamin,' said Goddard, clearly surprised. 'Why are you back here so soon?'

'Bless me Father for I have sinned.'

Goddard kissed the stole and replaced it on his shoulders. Mechanically he whispered, 'May the Lord be in your heart and on your lips that you may with truth and humility confess all your sins, in the name of the Father and of the Son and of the Holy Spirit. Amen.'

'It's me, Benji.'

'Yes Benji.'

'I have to confess to you that I have been very wicked.'

Goddard rolled his eyes. 'What have you done now?' He rubbed his hands distractedly over his face. 'Well, go on.'

Benji's voice filtered into the small stone chamber, soft and strangely deadly. Goddard bent his ear closer to the partition.

'You probably won't believe me after the practical joke with the scarecrow but that was only testing your reaction to things. You see, I was forced to take certain steps ...'

'Certain steps, Stanfield? What is this melodramatic nonsense?'

'No nonsense, Father. Believe me, it was like a nightmare. You see, what I told you as a joke, really did happen. I killed Charlie.'

'What?' cried Goddard in protest. 'What is this—another outrageous trick?'

'Honest to God, I'm not playing. I have a slingshot I keep hidden. It's tremendously powerful and my aim is deadly. He was already badly injured by the beating the police gave him and made an easy target. When he was done, he moved a little. He seemed to recognise me. He cursed us, me, you, the Church, I finished him off.'

The three bells of the consecration sounded in the chapel. Goddard could barely contain his rage but the great moment of the mass enforced silence.

'How can you behave this way to me, boy, when I was merciful to you and didn't expel you as every instinct prompted me to do? How can you?'

'I know it's hard to believe, specially after my previous confession, but it's true. I beg you to believe me.'

Goddard was shaking, becoming quite distraught. 'Satan has possessed your mind. You are very ill, my child. That is the only explanation. You are too ill to know what you are saying.'

'I know what I'm saying and I know what I've done.'

'Benjamin, please ...'

'It's no trick, Father ... I only ... it was ...' He broke into tears. 'I'm frightened Father, help me. I have killed a man.'

But Goddard had stopped listening. He was chattering to himself. 'I don't know what it is that compels you to play these hideous tricks, but one thing is certain. They can no longer be tolerated. You obviously have a deep and abiding resentment against me which makes our relationship impossible. I can't possibly continue to have any association with you. Go ... go ...'

'I need absolution, Father.'

'Absolution! For what? For lying? For tricks? For wilfully

abusing the sacraments?' He was on his feet now, standing by the door.

'For murder, Father. For killing Charlie.'

'I don't believe you, Benjamin. I can't.'

'You must,' he insisted. 'What would be the point of playing the same trick twice? I have killed. I need absolution.'

'I cannot give absolution for what I know is another practical joke, boy.'

'I swear by God Almighty and the hope I have of Heaven that it is true. I can give you proof.'

'Benji, Benji,' whined the anguished priest.

'About three hundred paces from where you found the scarecrow, in a straight line due North, there is a great tree. You can't miss it. It's huge, with exposed roots. I made his grave there—he's tucked up tight, inside, among the roots, covered with dirt and leaves.'

'I will hear no more of this, Benjamin. No more, not a word.' He left the confessor's room and headed towards the sacristy. He knelt at the open door and heard the end of the mass. When it was over, Father Keenan and two young servers entered. Goddard assisted them to divest, in a perfunctory manner. Eventually Keenan asked gently, 'Are you all right, Father?'

'All right? Oh, yes . . .' he replied.

'You must be feeling the strain of all the extra work. You should have asked me to take the confessions this afternoon. It is usually a very quiet duty.' Goddard almost laughed, and walked out into the chapel.

Some of the small congregation remained. Arthur was busy saying his twenty-five Hail Marys. Benjamin was standing by him, trying to talk to him. Goddard stormed down the aisle towards them. Realising he was in trouble, Benjamin dropped to his knees in an attitude of piety. Goddard informed him in no uncertain terms that if he wished to pray he was to do it alone. He motioned him to the farthest side of the chapel. Then he turned his attention to Arthur.

'You are not to associate with Stanfield. Do you understand? Avoid his company.' Startled, Arthur looked up. The warning was repeated, and Goddard left the chapel.

The past and present principals sat together in their office.

Goddard poured them both a glass of pale dry sherry. He handed Rivers his, and began.

'One of the boys is using the confessional as a weapon against me in a series of grotesque practical jokes—you appreciate my position, I cannot be more specific.'

'You should not be hearing the school confessions, Richard.'

'I do not as a rule, but I did make exceptions where I felt it was warranted.'

Rivers looked at him closely. 'The worst experience I have ever had was a very brief encounter at the English Church in Rome, just after the war, when an American soldier used it as a urinal—quite unintentionally, of course. I don't think he meant it as an expression of lavatorial humour.'

'Father, please.' Goddard fumbled in his soutane, took out a packet of cigarettes and lit himself one.

'I'm sorry, Richard. Do these practical jokes take you in? I find it highly unlikely.'

'Yes. I was fooled this once.'

'Strange. I'd have thought with your experience, it would have been difficult to deceive you.'

Goddard crushed out the cigarette. 'Well, this is not the normal run of mischief, I assure you. Something deeply wicked is moving the boy. I am convinced that part of his motivation is to destroy my authority.'

'Then you must destroy his first.' With that one sharp statement Father Rivers seemed transformed from a senile old eccentric with chronic bronchitis into a Jesuit worthy of Goddard's respect.

'Thank you, Father.'

'Richard, I am travelling across to a splendid restaurant in Bath this evening. A car is picking me up in an hour. Come with me—the break will do you the world of good. You'll enjoy the company—an old sparring partner of mine. A fearsome atheist when he was younger. He's now a writer—quite successful—whom age and the death of his son have mellowed into an agnostic.'

Goddard accepted. The idea of a good meal, diverting company and a little distance between himself and Sommerbury seemed a very good notion.

It was well after midnight when he returned from the feast

in good spirits. He saw Father Rivers to bed and strolled back to his apartment. The *truite farcee* had been superb, and, as Rivers had promised, the conversation had been diverting. The frustration and fury of the day had disappeared.

He halted under the covered archway to look out across the fields to Basket Wood. A Hunter Moon stood in the calm sky, sharply delineating the black trees. All was quiet.

Once in his apartment he changed out of his suit coat and trousers, donned a soutane and settled down to read himself to sleep. Then, with sudden decision, he took his cape from behind the door and walked out through the sleeping dormitory into the night.

He tramped across the field, a bizarre and lonely figure with his cape swirling behind him. At the edge of the clearing, he stopped. Night animals called, and scuttled about his feet—maybe just an adventurous water-rat. 'Oh God,' he murmured, 'I *can't* believe it.' He turned away and began walking back. He stopped again. 'Dear Jesus, let it not be true.' With renewed determination he headed deep into the wood, towards the place where he had found the scarecrow. In the moonlight, it was relatively easy. He found the spade he had thrown down in anger the night before. He scraped aimlessly around with it. 'Oh my good angel, whom God by his divine mercy has appointed to be my guardian, enlighten and protect me, direct and govern me this night.'

As he had been told, some yards away was the vast tree. He scratched among the roots with the spade, but met little success. He knelt and crawled into the womb beneath, scrabbling in the soft leafy earth with his hands. Deeper and deeper clawed his nails; trickles of soil fell from above. Suddenly he felt something. He scraped away the leaves, his hands tracing a coiled foetus-like form. No ...

He tried to back out of the terrible hole, to crawl away, like a blind crab. Outside he stood. He tried to run. After a few steps, he tripped and fell, and there he lay, his head pressed against the cool night earth, fighting to recover himself.

Eventually he rose, trembling, and slowly returned to the grave. He pulled the corpse free and dragged it into the moonlight. Gently he began to wipe the soil from the body. He could vaguely see the dark thick line of blood stretching from Blakey's ear and temple down the side of his neck. He took off his cape and wrapped it around the stark white body. For a long time he knelt there with the dead boy in his arms à Pieta.

Finally he gathered himself together. 'Oh God, whose nature is ever to show mercy, I humbly entreat thee for the soul of thy servant, this boy, who has departed this world. Do not deliver him into the enemy's hands, or put him out of mind forever, but bid thy holy angels welcome him and lead him home to paradise. Let him not undergo the pains of Hell because he died unshriven, but established him in that bliss which knows no ending. Through Christ Our Lord. Amen.' He said the prayer in one breath, inhaled deeply, then gave a long and desperate sigh, the breath forming a sound, a name.

'Benji, Benji, Benji, what have you done?'

He wrapped the body completely in the cloak and buried it where he had found it, beneath the tree, the head directly below the trunk. It made a perfect sepulchre for the Woodland King.

Then he retraced his steps in a daze, and hunched towards the sleeping school.

Part Five

ACTS OF CONTRITION

The birds were deep in conversation by the time the weary priest staggered into the courtyard. Morning light was beginning to shape the corridors as he moved towards the dormitory. He was about to cross the top corridor to Lacey House when he was met by Arthur, fully-dressed and carrying a pile of books. On seeing this early riser he pulled himself together.

'What are you doing up this early, boy?'

'I'm going to serve the first Mass, Father. I don't want to be late. Last night it was so dreaful. Benjamin was furious because you forbade me to associate with him. There was a fearful row in Lacey House and Father Roberts had to be called in. Benjamin hit me across the face—look.' He took off his glasses and showed where he had mended them with sellotape. 'The blow broke my glasses.'

Goddard seemed oblivious to shock. Nothing Benjamin did any more could surprise him.

'Oh, don't blame Benji,' continued Arthur, 'he's told me plenty of times I get on his nerves.'

Goddard felt nothing for Arthur and it was quite absurd to pretend he did, but on that vague grey morning he tried to encourage some intimacy. 'You are carrying books. Do you study at this hour?'

'If I am awake, Father, I read. Ancient Rome is my favourite at present. Did you realise that if a piece of cake fell out of a chicken's beak on the wrong side, the augurers wouldn't allow the army to fight?'

The priest stopped him—neither time nor circumstances favoured a discussion of classical superstitions. 'Arthur, would you do me a favour?'

It was as though the Archangel Gabriel had requested his assistance. 'Of course, Father. What can I do for you?'

'Is Benjamin serving the mass this morning?'

'Yes Father.'

'Oh my God . . . Never mind. Have you a pencil?' Arthur obliged. 'Paper?' Arthur looked apologetic. Goddard took one of the books and tore the library card out of it. He scribbled a note, folded it, and handed it to the boy, who received it with more detachment than bewilderment.

'Take this to the dormitory. Don't make any fuss. Give it to Stanfield. Wake him if necessary. Do not engage him in any conversation. Insist that it is important to follow the instructions. If he is difficult ask Sackville or Cawley to help you.'

Arthur hesitated. Goddard seemed about to speak again. Then they went their separate ways, Goddard making for the chapel.

He fell on his knees at the communion rail. The darkened chapel was illuminated only by the sanctuary light. The slow filter of morning was only just beginning to chase away the strange writhing shapes and shadows that attended its constant vigil.

'If I could—oh Jesus, forgive me—if I could only speak. Jesus, Jesus, Jesus, enlighten me with spiritual wisdom, grant me grace to benefit the souls of others by my good example, and to win back to thee by good counsel those souls who cannot come to thee, being heavy with sin.'

The heartfelt plea ended, he went into the sacristy and down the small stone corridor to the confessor's chamber. He sank into the chair and prayed silently, utter exhaustion taking its toll. Once he nearly fell asleep, but Benji's voice, eerie and distant, drew attention to his present cares.

'You sent for me Father,' a sleepy voice came through the partition.

Slowly and with great effort Goddard chose his words and replied, 'Benji, you have committed a terrible mortal sin. A crime that is punishable not only by God but by law.'

'I couldn't help it Father, I couldn't bear him to leave me, to go off with other people.'

'You couldn't bear him to enjoy his life so you took it away from him.'

'Father, help me back to God's grace. Only with His help

will I be able to resist the things that made me do wrong.'

'What sort of things, my son?'

'The rage ... the terrible crippling rage that comes over me. The fear of having no one to ...'

'Love you?' interrupted Goddard. 'Tell me about your rage.'

'I don't remember much. I only know when it's coming over me. I feel hot and lose control and I want to hurt someone. I enjoy thinking of different ways to hurt people. Once I just imagined torture. I even enjoyed the idea of it happening to me. But now it's not in my head. It's physical. The temptation is to hurt people physically. God help me. The temptation is to kill again.'

The admission was like a push into the face, almost hurling Goddard up out of his seat. 'Benji—Benjamin—what did you say?'

'Kill again. Other boys. Dowd—he's probably my only real adversary—or Arthur. He's so weak and clinging. He never leaves me alone. I despise him so much I want to stamp on him, trample him under my foot. Ugly weedy little cripple.'

It was as if Benjamin's voice had hands that were clawing their way through the grille to twist the purple stole about Goddard's neck. The horror choked him. 'You mean kill again? You want to kill Arthur?'

'I don't mean to, Father. I will strive with all my will not to, but I can't pretend the temptation isn't there. Don't you realise, it was the most exciting thing I ever did?'

Goddard pressed his ear to the grille to catch every whispered word, so close that confessing mouth and receiving ear might almost touch. 'Exciting,' he whispered, voice crackling with terror, 'you found murder exciting?'

'Surely you understand that, Father? Killing makes you powerful, suddenly you're in charge. It's a strange feeling, but it doesn't last long. When I killed Charlie, I had an orgasm without even touching myself.'

Goddard turned away from the voice and rubbed his ear. It was as though the most cruel thorns were being driven into his brain. He wet his bottom lip and dryly swallowed to make saliva. In his hands the Rosary beads moved constantly as he fought to stop himself breaking down.

'Father, I only tell you my deepest secrets because I know

125

that, of all the people I've ever known, you are the only one who would understand. You must have wanted to kill someone, sometime, if only for a moment, in a temper.'

This jerked the priest from his transfixed silence. 'No. Not even for a moment. Satan is in you,' he cried out.

'Father!'

'Benjamin, my son, I must help you.'

'Father!' came the anguished voice. 'Help me to resist. Lead me to God. Absolve me.'

'I will give you absolution. Only God can heal your soul now. I cannot keep you from Him. You will say a twenty-four hour penance of prayer. One Rosary every hour—the five sorrowful mysteries. Think on each carefully as you pray. Pray also for the repose of the soul of your victim, your lost friend. Make yourself available to God's forgiveness.'

'But will He, Father? Will he forgive this great sin?'

Goddard drew himself up and spoke, for the first time, with pride and certainty. 'Benji, there is no unpardonable sin, provided the sinner repents, provided his heart is truly contrite. Of this I am certain. In this certainty, I pledge my life. The fallen angels cannot win back grace, but fallen man can recover grace, through a man who, in this sacrament of the confessional, possesses greater power than was ever given to God's angels. Trust me. I bring you to God's forgiveness. Do you trust me? Answer me, Stanfield.'

'Of course, Father.'

'I thank God. Benji, begin the Act of Contrition.' Goddard raised his hand, still dirty from the grave, and made the sign of the cross. The Act of Contrition was said. He gave his absolution. 'My child, you have entered a dark region of your life, a region of evil. You must turn back before Satan claims you utterly. But I will help you. Now go in peace and say your penance. We shall during the morning go together to the police.'

'Go to the police?'

'Of course. They must be informed as soon as possible. You have made your peace with God for the sin, now you must answer to the Law. Realise that conditions are on your side; that Blakey was a known criminal, a corrupter of youth. You will claim self-defence.'

'No. I will do penance, Father, in the hope that it will help me to overcome the temptation to kill again, but I don't think I will go to the police. They are certain to put me inside. I would hate that. No. I won't go to the police. And of course, we know *you* can't.'

'Benjamin ...' No reply came; the boy had left the confessional. Goddard remained, his hand pressed against the grille. He looked as if he had been turned to stone.

'Dear God, the temptation is to kill again. Dowd, Arthur ... Oh God help us ...'

Back in his apartments, Goddard washed and prepared himself for the day. He attempted to collate the English examination answers into the order he would return them, but his trembling hands prevented him. He prayed again for guidance. Sinking into the soft body of the chair, he fell asleep ... in a beautiful cathedral, much older now, celebrating Mass. He turns. Assisting him is Father Benjamin Stanfield. He leans across to embrace him; 'Pax vobiscum.' The beautiful young priest gags him with his stole, twisting and turning it till the cross covers Goddard's face. The terrified priest looks to his congregation for help, but sees only Arthur, approaching the communion rails. Benji walks forward as if to dispense the sacrament. Arthur innocently kneels. Benji draws the knife— the kneeling boy with eyes closed and mouth open to receive the sacrament, oblivious to the danger. Unable to warn him, Goddard struggles helplessly. Benji comes nearer and nearer the communion rail; Arthur protrudes his tongue slightly to receive the wafer. Benjamin plunges the knife down into the hapless boy's mouth. He turns, the white and gold chasuble steaming with gore. Benjamin, now like an Aztec priest, pokes his tongue out at Goddard, insolent, haunting, demonic ...

Goddard woke abruptly from the nightmare to find Benjamin leaning over him. 'I'm sorry to wake you, Father, but class has started. There's been changes to the morning's programme. Here are the notes from Father Moore with the details.'

Goddard stared, appalled. Benjamin smiled his half-smile and silently left the room.

Some excuse had been made: Father Goddard's morning

periods were transferred to after lunch. In the senior class-room, a large group of boys lounged about, anticipating the long-awaited English results. Someone had prepared a little surprise for God. In addition to the main blackboard at the front of the room, a smaller movable one stood by the door. It bore a chalk sketch of a priest with a halo and angel's wings. This mythical figure, this winged Goddard, flew above a swamp. Among the trees beneath him lurked a hand, holding a hunter's rifle which was exploding towards him. The caption read, 'Crow Hunting Season Open.'

Benjamin arrived. 'Where have you been this morning?' asked Sackville.

'None of your business. Hey,' he said, catching sight of the blackboard, 'that's good. Who did it?'

'I dunno,' mumbled Peterson, 'I thought it was one of your efforts.'

Benjamin grabbed a fistful of sweets that Manning was trying to conceal and hurled them around the room. The boys scrambled for them. 'What are you doing, Benjamin?'

'Saving you from a heart attack in later life.'

From the back of the room, Bryce shouted, 'Who is leaving library books around? I've spent months trying to organise the library.' He held the book above his head, trying to spot the culprit. 'Come on Raphaels, it's bound to be you. You're so vague.'

'Not me ...'

'What's it called?' enquired Cawley.

'I, Claudius.'

'I clawed his what?' said Dowd.

'I Claudius,' came the librarian's tart reply. 'You know, the lame Emperor. He was on the Beeb.'

'I'll bet it's Arthur,' mused Benjamin, 'Veni, Vidi, Vici. I limped, I twitched, I dribbled.'

Benjamin began a cruel imitation of Arthur—Goddard saw enough of it through the glass panels of the door. As he entered past the movable blackboard, Sackville moved behind him to revolve the offending drawing from sight. Goddard stared at Benjamin.

'I was just giving my version of Claudius the God ...'

'I know what you were doing. And what are you doing with that board, Sackville?'

'Nothing, Father.'

'Sit down.'

'Someone said the day's programme had been changed. I heard that the English papers weren't being returned,' said Sackville, prevaricating.

'Changed?' roared Goddard. 'What are you babbling about?'

'Sorry, Father.' He returned to his place.

The sleepless and haggard priest took his place in front of the class. On the floor, before the small blackboard, he saw a sweet. He walked over and picked it up.

'Manning,' he intoned dryly, and held the sweet above his head. The movement caught the revolving surface of the board, and it edged slowly round to reveal a little of the drawing. Raphaels gasped audibly. Goddard looked at him, made no comment, and returned to his rostrum.

'In spite of disquieting rumours to the contrary, I know you will all be relieved to hear that the results are about to descend upon you.'

A mock groan rose from the class, but was quickly silenced by the priest, who made the Sign of the Cross. Although puzzled by this afternoon prayer, the boys stood to pray with him.

'In the Name of the Father and of the Son and of the Holy Ghost, Amen. A morning offering to Our Lord,' the boys exchanged amused glances, 'that all our effort and struggle today be in his name. To St Anthony of Padua, whose feast it is tomorrow, we dedicate our work today, in the hope that his fine example will guide us and keep us attentive and alert. Let us also pray for the repose of the soul of Oh—' Every boy looked up. Goddard had remembered Blakey's name. Out of nowhere, he had remembered the barbarian's name. He was actually praying for the repose of his soul in front of the startled boys. Luckily he prevented the name from escaping, unthinkingly substituting, 'Father Rivers.'

'Let us pray for the repose of the soul of Father Rivers,' he repeated.

'He's not dead yet, Father,' said Benjamin, who should have known, having spent some of the morning in the sprightly old man's company.

Goddard hit the roof. 'I know very well he's not. Don't

you think I would be the first to know a thing like that? In the Name of the Father and of the Son and of the Holy Ghost, Amen. In future, never, I repeat, never, interrupt prayers unless it is a matter of the gravest importance.'

'But ...'

'Don't answer back.' He took a long sheet of paper from a folder on the desk. 'Don't try my patience, boy. Watch yourself.' On the scroll were the columns where the boys had been asked to enter their results. 'Bryce. Why haven't I any results from Geography?'

'Well, I haven't got it back yet Father.'

'Everyone else has. Why are you the exception?'

'Well, the Brig—Brigadier Bryce-Jones said he must have mislaid it. You see, I answered in a pink folder, not a blue one, and he might have got it mixed up with the pink, which is the colour for science answers.'

'I'm not interested in excuses, boy. Dyson, is there any reason why you have not managed to fill in your results from yesterday? I'm sure we can expect a colourful explanation.'

There was no answer.

'Arthur,' said Goddard sharply.

He looked up.

'Where's Arthur? Have any of you seen him?'

No one replied. His voice rose, becoming shriller. 'Come on. One of you must have seen him.'

'He hasn't been around at all today, Father,' said Sackville.

'Why wasn't I told? Why didn't someone tell me immediately?'

'He was in the library last night,' said a voice.

'No, I saw him this morning just after Mass,' said another.

'And no one has seen him since?'

There was a further silence. None of the boys seemed particularly concerned. With a visible effort Goddard brought himself to meet the one gaze he had so far avoided.

'Do you know of his whereabouts?'

So deliberate and loaded was the question that Benjamin almost smiled. His lips curled to cover it as he replied. 'I don't ... really ...'

The priest turned white. He swayed. He clutched the blackboard to save himself from falling. It spun to reveal the cartoon. The boys froze, terrified of the explosion it would evoke, especially given the violent state the priest was in.

Goddard failed to notice it.

'A search must be made of the school. Now. The whole school. The grounds. You know his haunts. Off you go.'

'Now?' asked Cawley. 'Surely he'll turn up. He spends a lot of time by himself.'

'Now, now, now, do I make myself clear?'

The group dispersed. Last to leave was Benjamin. Goddard tried to ignore him, but against his better judgement, asked, 'Where are you going?'

'To look for Arthur, Father.'

Goddard did not look at him, but pressed on. 'Have you nothing to say to me?'

'Say to you? What about?'

Again horror swept over the priest. Benjamin looked coolly back at him. This over-reaction amused him.

'Excuse me Father.' He left the room.

Goddard also moved into the corridor, but did not pursue him, heading instead in the opposite direction, towards the administration offices. On the way, he met Father Roberts.

'Oh Father, you were supervisor last night.'

'Yes.'

'I believe you had some trouble with my house.'

'Nothing worth reporting, Father Goddard. I merely separated the two fellows I felt were responsible.'

'Who were they?'

'Stanfield and er ...'

'Dyson. Arthur Dyson.'

'Yes. He went off to the Common Room or the library— I'm not sure which.'

'Have you seen him since?'

'No ...'

'So I was the last to see him, except for Benjamin,' said Goddard to himself. Aloud, he continued, 'Have you any idea where he might be?'

'Not off hand. He's not a popular lad and spends lots of time alone. There are plenty of places around the school ... Excuse me Father, but I must get on.'

'Yes, of course.' Father Roberts made to move on. 'Before you go, Father, I'd like a quick word about Stanfield.'

'Benjamin? Has he anything to do with this?' Roberts

avoided mentioning the notorious joke directly.

'I don't know. What was he doing to Arthur last night?'

'Just teasing that got out of hand. You know Stanfield better than I, Father—full of the devil,' said the priest, with an affectionate smile.

'Full of the Devil,' replied Goddard gravely.

'I'll organise some of my fellows to help. I'm sure he'll be found.' With a puzzled look Roberts continued on his way.

'Found, yes—but alive?' said Goddard to himself, despairingly. He fumbled nervously with the rosary beads in his pocket. Suddenly he broke into a run. In the main foyer he met Miss Froggatt, the school secretary.

'Ah there you are, Father—the timetable said you were in Room D36.'

'Not now, Miss Froggatt, I'm rather pre-occupied.'

'Father, I've just received a call from Rainer's mother. She wants to pick him up on Tuesday, not the Wednesday as planned. If he can't stay on here, he's to go with Cawley to stay at Bristol.'

'What on earth has this to do with me, woman? Speak to Father Moore.'

'But Father Moore said that you ...'

Goddard had disappeared from view into the main drive. He circled the buildings, frantically searching for somewhere Arthur might hide.

Dowd, Gregory and Black, who were ostensibly on the hunt for the missing boy, were sitting behind the garden shed puffing luxuriously on a cigarette. Almost before they realised it, Goddard was on top of them. Black hurriedly stubbed out the evidence. All three stood as Goddard approached them.

'Aw shit, he saw us,' whispered Dowd.

'Well, is this helping to find Dyson? Have you seen Stanfield?'

'What ... out here, Father?' Dowd was still nervously awaiting punishment for smoking.

'No, in China. Of course out here.' Goddard sighed with exasperation and stormed off, leaving the three astonished smokers to continue.

'I've only got one more,' cautioned Black, 'so keep an eye out.' No sooner was it lit when Goddard made his second appearance.

'Not again,' moaned Black. Gregory was about to throw the offending article away, but Black took it from him and cupped it in his hands.

'Are you sure you haven't seen Stanfield? This is one of his regular haunts, is it not? Think, fellows, ransack the dim recesses of those craniums. Black—what about you?'

'Well, yes Father, I saw him ...' he pondered. 'No, sorry ... I ... Wait, Father, weren't Dyson and Stanfield together just before breakfast. They were walking together across the field.'

'... towards the wood?' asked Goddard.

'I didn't take much notice,' apologised Black.

Gregory broke in helpfully, 'Father, Benjamin spends a lot of time doing the masters' garden, with Father Pollard.'

Goddard left them and sped back towards the school. 'What's up with him?' asked Black.

'Are you sure you saw Dyson and Stanfield together this morning?'

'I'm not sure, but it's got rid of God for the moment, and besides, this cigarette was starting to burn my hand.'

Goddard found Benjamin, en route for the masters' garden, being given instructions about a certain patch of roses by Father Pollard. Goddard interrupted.

'Would you excuse me a moment, Father, I must speak to Benjamin.' Benjamin greeted him warmly.

'You're not out looking for Dyson.'

'Why should I? I wanted to work in the garden.'

Goddard swayed a little. 'Did you spend any time with him this morning?'

'I saw him early. I was going to take a run across the wood.'

The very mention of the wood was agony—the priest could say no more. To mention—even indirectly—things he could only know from those murderous confessions would be mortal sin. He turned on his heel and left. Father Pollard resumed his instruction.

He paced his burgundy office in a fury of indecision. Through the window he could see Benjamin, now alone, prospecting beneath a rose-tree with his spade. It was too much for him. He leapt into the outer office, and with a fierce, sudden gesture, smashed the glass of the fire alarm. Bells, hooters and sirens throughout the old manor called out their warning.

The school began to empty. Goddard ran to the foyer. He collided with a large pile of papers borne by Miss Froggatt, which flew in all directions. He helped her to her feet, and they began retrieving the papers, shouting apologies at each other above the din of the alarms. Rescue came in the form of Father Mountjoy, marching a file of junior boys through to safety.

'Keep those lines straight—no need to hurry,' he instructed the leaders. The file of blue blazers enabled Goddard to make a break from the secretary, out into the drive, where the serried ranks of the community were assembling.

Mrs Hoskins was indulging a panic. 'They are saying it started in my kitchen, in the chip pan, Father. It isn't true.' He looked at her uncomprehendingly and pushed on into the mustering forms. Within ten minutes the entire school was assembled. Masters, prefects and House Captains began checking the babbling crowd. Father Moore arrived with Father Rivers. Moore had brought a large plan of the school and the central register.

'There's nothing in the labs, Father,' announced Roberts.

'The kitchen is clear and safe,' emphasised Mrs Hoskins.

'Absolutely nothing,' called Brigadier Bryce-Jones, as he brought his platoon of fire-scouts into the drive.

'Thank you, Brigadier,' said Moore. Voices began to chime above the babble.

'Lower Five Beta. All present.'

'Lead on,' replied Moore. The group broke ranks and returned to the school.

'Three Alpha, all present.'

'Lead on.'

And so on, until a shrill voice cried, 'We're missing twelve from Francis Five.'

'They're on an outing to Berkely Castle,' Miss Froggatt advised Moore.

'Well, Father Moore, this has been a pleasant waste of a half-hour,' said the Brigadier, 'but I wish you had informed my lot there was to be a fire drill.'

'It was not a fire-drill, Brigadier, one of the alarms must

have short-circuited. Get your fire group together and find out which one.'

'Father Moore, we have two missing from Lacey Alpha.'

'Who's that?' asked Moore. Goddard moved closer.

'Stanfield, Benjamin ...' Goddard knew where he was ... 'Dyson, Arthur.' His worst fears were confirmed.

'Both in your house, Richard,' said Moore.

'I know where Stanfield is, Father. He is in the garden. I'll deal with him.'

'Dyson?' enquired Father Rivers.

'Perhaps he's fallen,' suggested Moore, 'Hardy, get some prefects and have a look round for Arthur Dyson. He may have had trouble with his leg.'

Goddard was already heading determinedly for the principal's office.

On his way there he could see Benjamin at work in the rose-garden. He had stripped to the waist and hung the shirt from his belt. His normally tidy hair was tousled into curls from running his sweaty, dirty hands through it. The final defiance —a cigarette balanced behind one ear. Goddard found the sight deeply worrying and offensive—the young god of Sommerbury now consciously taking on the attributes of his newer hero. Around his neck he wore the cross that Father Pollard had given to Blakey.

Goddard could contain himself no longer. To see this lovely boy aping the style of his victim, a frightening indication of the state of his mind. He approached him.

'I think it's about time we faced this together.'

'What have I—'

'No prevarications please. We must talk this thing out— now!'

'What thing, Father?'

Goddard walked a few paces into deeper seclusion. Benjamin put down his tools and followed him.

'A few days ago, you gave me permission to refer to what you said to me in confession. I will take that liberty again— only with your permission.'

'Of course.' Benjamin beamed at him.

Goddard moved the boy closer to the wall, out of sight of any chance passer-by.

'Very well, Benjamin. You must tell me truthfully—have you harmed Arthur?'

Benjamin looked puzzled. 'Me, Father?' he said, with wide-eyed innocence. 'Father, why are you picking on me? I thought it was all over.'

'Benjamin, don't make this more difficult than it is already. You murdered Charlie. You confessed the experience excited you . . . you even hinted that . . .'

'Father,' he broke in, 'you know that was only a joke.'

'A joke! What do you say, a joke, you vile creature, a joke? I have seen his body. You told me where to look.'

Benjamin remained cool. 'You must be having hallucinations, Father. I sent you to find a scarecrow, don't you remember?'

'I tell you, I have seen the body.'

'That's impossible. We both know he's gone. You must be ill, Father. I don't mean to be disrespectful, but perhaps a doctor . . .'

Goddard lost control and slapped Benjamin hard across the face. 'Bold as brass. How dare you speak to me like that. You stand there a self-confessed murderer, a cowardly brutish boy who beat in the head of his best friend with a rock and tell me—'

The humiliating slap loosed Benjamin's temper. 'You'd better see a psychiatrist, Father. Maybe you're feeling guilty about sending the police in to bash Blakey.'

Goddard choked. 'Guilty? Why should I feel guilty?'

'Well, you were the one who was responsible for breaking up our friendship, you were the one who caused the most hurt, you must be ill to make all these wild accusations against me.'

'Liar!' Again the hand cut across the boy's cheek.

Benjamin had had enough. 'Hardy's father's a headshrinker, Father, better ring him now before you become dangerous. They know all about the problems of celibate priests.'

'Cain! Cain!' howled the priest. 'Stop your mouth.' He reeled, then regained a partial grip on himself. 'Your tricks, your insolence won't drive me mad, if that's what you're after, you young blackguard. The Devil is in you, I see the fiend dancing behind those eyes of yours. He won't bring me down. I'm well equipped to fight the Devil. You have a worthy opponent here. Remember that!'

Benjamin was apparently appalled by this outburst. He also found the man's behaviour quite comic, but hid his amusement in tones of sweet reason.

'Father, please stop. Please calm yourself and listen to me rationally.'

'Rationally? So it is the sweet voice of reason, is it? Satan appears in many disguises to provoke and unstring, but you don't deceive me. I'll be constant,' he went on, babbling furiously to himself, oblivious to Benjamin, 'Jesus, Jesus, Jesus, make me constant in Faith, Hope and Charity, let no false delight of this deceitful world blind me, no fleshly temptation or fraud of the Devil shake my heart.'

Benjamin had to bite his cheeks so as not to burst out laughing, but the mirth was swept away by fear as the ghastly priest turned and confronted him again.

'Benjamin, the fiend stands in your face, he peeps out of your eyes, this way and that way, like a skulking squirrel. It's turn and turn about—the bewilderment of the babe, the bright cunning of the serpent.'

Benji turned and fled from the garden, across the fields and into the wood. Goddard watched him. 'There is no hiding place, my dear son. Stay. I will help you,' he murmured. He regained his composure and returned to his office. The afternoon was nearly over.

Father Moore placed a slip of paper on the desk in front of him. 'That is Arthur's mother's telephone number. I think you should phone her.'

'Yes. I will do so.'

'Richard—the alarm that was broken was in my office.'

'Yes. I raised the alarm. I needed to confirm my fears about Dyson.'

'So you actually expected him to be absent?'

'Yes. Yes, I did.'

'It seems a rather expensive and elaborate way of confirming your fears.' Goddard just looked at him. 'Richard, what is all this? You have been behaving very strangely.'

Goddard shivered. 'Even if I could ... there simply aren't words to describe ... things, forces. I mean ...'

'It doesn't matter. I have asked the local police to let us know

137

if they hear anything. I've looked at Dyson's record, though. He has a curious habit of going off by himself.'

Goddard wasn't listening. He shouted at the other priest with sudden vehemence, 'I shall handle this matter, Father Moore.'

'Of course, Father, but—'

'There can be no but. Only obedience.' And quietly, to himself, 'My wounds fester and rankle.'

Moore wasn't sure what he had said. 'I beg your pardon, Father?'

'Nothing. Nothing. Leave me now.' Moore slowly made for the door.

'My whole frame afire. My body diseased. So spent, so crushed, I groan aloud in the weariness of my heart,' murmured Goddard. Moore turned and looked at him enquiringly.

'Father, are you all right? You seem burdened, uneasy . . .'

'Michael, I am perfectly all right. I need to be alone for a while. There is so much to do.'

'If you want to work on here, I'll have your dinner sent up.'

Goddard managed to smile a little. When the door finally closed he slumped into the chair with a deep groan.

Mrs Hoskins brought his dinner personally. She said nothing, but fussed over him sympathetically. She closed the bay windows and drew the curtains on the disappearing day.

The warm food seemed to give him strength for another effort at normality. He began reading the large pile of letters on his desk, signing some, referring others to Moore or Froggatt as the case required. At about ten-thirty, there was a knock at the door. Father Pollard rushed in.

'Father, I'm afraid I have some very terrible news.'

'News?' barked Goddard, 'what news?'

'Well,' said the old man, gasping for breath, 'I was in the chapel, and my eyes alighted on the foot of the rood-screen, where, all along, in little heaps, was, dear oh dear, sawdust.'

'What does this mean?' Goddard's mind raced.

'Well, I'm afraid it can only mean a visitation from our friend the woodworm, and indeed, on closer inspection, there were little holes, scarcely bigger than a pinprick.'

Goddard ran his hands through his hair. He listened patiently to the old priest and thanked him. Then he escorted him out of the door, assuring him that all would be carefully looked into at the first board meeting during the break. Father Pollard was grateful and thanked him for the moral and vocal support he was sure would be forthcoming. Once alone again, Goddard attempted to concentrate on the paperwork, but more and more his mind began to wander.

'Beaten down, bowed to the earth, I go mourning all day long. Despair stalks me like some hunting animal, a bright bird of prey...

> The owlet atheism
> Sailing on obscene wings athwart the moon
> Drops his blue-fringed lids and holds them close
> And hooting at the glorious sun in Heaven
> Cries out! Where is it?'

These ramblings were interrupted, the sound of the door locking. Goddard believed it was a knock. 'Yes? Come in?' There was a soft knock on the door.

'Well, what is it? Enter.'

There was no response. He moved across and tried the door. It was locked. Another knock, this time sharp and insistent. He recoiled as if he had received an electric shock.

'Who is it? Why is this door locked?' Goddard banged on it. 'I'm in here. Unlock this door.'

Then came the faint, almost inaudible whisper of Benjamin's voice.

'Please Father, I must confess.'

'Benjamin, why is this door locked? Open it this instant.' He shook the door.

'It will act as the confessional box, Father. In the name of the Father and of the Son and of the Holy Ghost, Amen. Bless me, Father, for I have sinned.'

'Benjamin, this is highly irregular.'

'I'm sorry I felt the need to deny everything when we met today, but I'm sure you realise my need to protect myself in public. Here in confession it's different. If I tell you something here, you can't talk about it. It's secret.' Goddard was pressed against the wood, trying desperately to catch each word.

'I must tell you about Arthur. He's dead. I killed him. That is why you couldn't find him.'

Goddard slumped to the floor, his body limp, as if drugged. 'No,' he cried, 'you couldn't murder Arthur.'

'He was the natural choice. You were very foolish to involve him this morning. He brought me your note. He knew something was going on. So I took him to the wood to explain my terrible position. Of course he didn't believe me, so I left it at that and went on to visit Blakey's grave. I wanted to ask his forgiveness. True to form, Arthur followed me. Well, you know what he's like, bleating like a little limping lamb. He found me kneeling by the big tree. I was crying. It was very moving, a sort of Requiem between Blakey and me. "What are you kneeling there for, Benji?"—you know how he goes on. "Why are you crying? Why are you talking to that tree as if it were Blakey?" He ruined the whole ceremony. I lost control and smashed his ugly head against the tree. Smashed and smashed and smashed.' The words disintegrated into hysterical sobs. Then the tears dried and the voice full of loathing continued the list of Arthur's shortcomings.

'He made himself so low. He made me cringe. I had to squash him, I had to stand on him, turn his face into the ground, little snotty scuttling crab.'

Goddard's voice was low and remote. 'The real reason you killed Arthur, Benji, is simple.'

'I don't understand, Father.'

'You said yourself that Arthur was aware of what was going on. You had involved him in your previous escapades. He was not bound to silence, like me. He could have told the police.' There was a long silence. Goddard had become very calm and very serious. He felt, for the first time in this whole episode, that he was at last beginning to get control.

'Having been absolved from the most hideous crime there is, you immediately celebrate it by committing another.' He rose to his feet, his voice returning to the reverberating stone it had once been.

'What do you want from me? I have no mind to absolve you, Benjamin.'

'I wasn't concerned about me, Father, only Arthur needs Extreme Unction. He's buried right next to Blakey, under the tree. I've left the spade I was using this afternoon in the rose-garden up against your bay window.'

Goddard heard the key being removed from the lock, then footsteps, then the key being turned in the outer door. Then there was silence. He sank to the floor, his head in his hands. 'Not up there again—oh God, help me.'

After a while, he walked over to the windows, drew the curtain, and pushed open the double door. A spade propped against it clattered to the ground.

A clear bright night filtered down through the canopy of branches as the priest walked the now familiar path into the deep wood. In the half-light it was clear that the grave had been touched since his last visit. In fact, the spade hit Arthur's brace almost immediately. There in a shallow grave above Blakey's body lay the second wretched victim. He knelt and prayed for the resurrection of Arthur's soul. His fingers recoiled in horror as he brushed the earth back over the grey-stockinged foot and protruding metal attachment. He knelt, resting the weight of his body on his heels. His hand touched Arthur's boot lying nearby.

He became aware of a presence above him. He crouched uncertainly as the figure moved like a shadow across the starry night sky.

'You! What do you want up there?' he gasped, despair and anguish overriding fear.

'I saw you coming up and I followed you. I wanted to be with you.' Goddard made no sound, no gesture. Benjamin went on, 'I wanted to apologise for my rudeness—you know, when you asked me about Arthur.'

Goddard looked at his tormentor aghast. He mutely proffered the boot to him.

'Well, I'm sorry,' said Benjamin, awkwardly, 'I shouldn't have said what I did. I lost my temper. I got carried away. You know what I'm like when I lose control.'

Goddard shook his head like a wounded animal, his agitation increasing with every step the boy took towards him. Benji was also uneasy and attempted to change the subject.

'What's this Father? It looks like a grave.'

'You know very well it's a grave. Please, Benji, don't torture me.' Benji gave him a slow confidential smile.

'I suppose we should tell your friends in blue. No, let's solve the mystery ourselves. What do you say? You can be Father Brown.' Benjamin made an elaborate show of inspecting the grave. 'You'll never pin this one on me, Father.'

With a great cry that carved the night Goddard rushed at him, brandishing the spade above his head.

'It is enough. You will torture me no more. You will kill no more. If I can't go to the police, I must stop you myself. It is the only way.'

Benjamin backed away from the mad priest, still playacting. Surprised by the dangerous advance he tripped over a long root and sprawled beneath the tree.

'Great darkness bore you hither and shall now carry you hence.'

Benjamin screamed. 'Father, Father.' But the pitiful pleas went unheeded. Goddard smashed the spade down into Benjamin's face, howling, 'Azræl! Azræl! Azræl!' Again and again he beat the dull muddy metal into the face of the boy, silencing forever that voice. The blood-choked screams ceased and the fury of the Warrior of God subsided, sobbing in a kind of ecstasy, his eyes pinioned to the sky.

'Oh God, see where he lies, Lucifer, cast down, his forked tongue between his teeth sopping up the dust. Oh my Lord, you have triumphed. He is extinguished.'

Gradually, a sense of another reality returned. His breathing slowed, his sobs dwindled, and the bloody weapon fell from his hand.

As if for the first time, he looked tenderly upon the broken face of Benjamin. He knelt and gathered him into his arms. His eyes were filled with tears, his hands stained with the boy's blood; he leant close and whispered in the dead ear.

'You were very close to me. The Devil chose you well for his work. But witness by my hand it has come to naught. Rest in peace, child. God will receive you.'

For the first and last time, he kissed the mortified, brutalised flesh, and quietly cried.

He carried the body like the holiest bundle and placed it in the shadowy bower, covered it with a layer of dirt and leaves, then walked towards the stream. Here he prostrated himself and washed. Reflected in the cool and silent stream, a pale dead moon looked up at him.

By the time he regained the school the moon was almost invisible in the pink and white light of the new morning. With great determination and effort he began a letter to his superior, Father Mackkerras. It made no reference to any of the events, only to his present bitter dilemma. It ended with a request for help. 'Counsel me,' he wrote, 'how best to walk out from the shadow of damnation in which I now stand, since I can no longer counsel myself. I require your immediate attention,

    I am yours in Christ,
      R. Goddard S.J.'

With tears and trembling hands he knelt before the cross on his desk.

'I am spent with sighing, till my skin clings to my bones. I am no better than a pelican out in the desert, an owl on some ruined dwelling. I keep watch, lonely as a single sparrow on the house-top. Still my enemies taunt me. Ashes are all my food. I drink nothing but what comes to me mingled with my own tears. I shrink before thy vengeful anger, so low hast thou brought me, who did once lift me so high.'

He reached across the desk and tore the letter to shreds. He fell asleep facing the small cross.

Part Six

DIES IRAE

Day of Wrath! Oh Day of Mourning
See fulfilled the prophets warning
Heaven and Earth in ashes burning

Cawley knocked cautiously at the door. Goddard awoke. He had spent the whole night on his knees.

'Come in,' he called, wiping the tear-stained sleep out of his eyes. He rose stiffly. Cawley entered with a tea tray and placed it on Goddard's desk, as the priest swept the remains of his note into the waste-paper basket.

'Good morning, Father, God bless you. Father Moore thought you might like to breakfast in here,' said the boy, with toothy good cheer.

'How kind. Thank you, Benji.'

Cawley looked astonished at the bedraggled priest. Goddard poured himself a cup of tea—he seemed very calm and not remotely distressed.

'I will be handing back those English papers first thing—a remarkable literature essay, Benji, you're a bright boy.'

'I'm Terry, Father. Terence Cawley.'

Goddard looked upon him, took a sip of tea, and agreed. 'Yes, you are.' Cawley left quickly.

Goddard crossed to the small hand basin, took a towel and wiped his face. Then he vigorously washed his hands in the running water, the mechanical wringing motions reminiscent of a ritual ablution before the consecration. He dried his hands, blessed himself and said a silent grace. Father Moore came in.

'You realise you had an early Mass this morning, Father Goddard.'

'God forgive me ... I ...' he held his head, his teeth chattered slightly— 'I ... I overslept.'

'You sound rather ill.'

'I'm perfectly well—maybe a slight chill. Change of season flu coming on, I expect.'

'Well, take it easy. Keenan said Mass. Will you take his evening Mass?'

'No. I am unable to do that, Michael.'

Father Moore was surprised, but did not press the matter. A priest would only refuse to say Mass in a dire circumstance. In this case, Goddard's mortal sin prevented him. Moore returned to the outer office where there was a large pile of letters on Froggatt's desk.

'Only one personal item—a parcel,' he called.

'Open it, please.'

'It's a book of Macaulay's poems. What ever for? We've got several in the library—show me.'

Goddard gave the book a cursory glance. He was about to put it down when one dog-eared page caught his attention. Absent-mindedly he opened the book there. His eyes fell immediately to a stanza marked with red ink. It was a refrain from the Battle of Lake Regillus:

> *'Those trees in whose dim shadow*
> *The ghastly priest doth reign*
> *The priest who slew the slayer*
> *and shall himself be slain.'*

With a sharp cry he hurled the offending book from his hand as if it had come alive and bitten him.

'Is this some idea of a joke?' he shouted.

Moore ran in to see Goddard reel, about to fall to the floor, and caught him just in time. Goddard leant with one hand on the desk to support himself.

'Father, you are not well. Please sit down.'

He sat, but within seconds leaped to his feet, staring wildly out at Basket Wood. 'Benji, I thought I saw . . .'

'Saw what?'

'A child. A boy I know. He's gone though. Heaven will welcome him.'

'Sit down, Father, please.'

He sat again. Moore took some tea from the tray and helped

146

him sip it slowly. Goddard looked up at him kindly.

'Thank you for the drink. It was a sudden turn.'

'Might I suggest you go upstairs and rest?'

'Rest?' said Goddard, almost childishly. 'No, there will be time enough for that all too soon.' He sighed deeply and stared at the book lying on the floor, the sunlight creeping slowly towards it. Moore hovered uncertainly. Goddard sighed again. 'I am snared about. Like a tapering shadow, my days dwindle.'

'Father, please, either collect yourself or allow me to phone a doctor. Please take the day off.'

'No, I will be ready for the day in a moment, Michael. Thank you for your concern.'

Moore left him.

> *Lo! The book exactly worded*
> *Wherein all hath been recorded*
> *Thence shall judgement be awarded*

Father Goddard arrived in the classroom exactly on time, not the shattered man who had met the day, but again the giant who had ruled Sommerbury for years. The old God was back, shaven and clean, and wearing his soutane with the razor-sharp pleats; the granite fortress-face was as impervious as ever, giving no hint of the deep and crippling agony of the past few days. The papers were on the desk where he had left them. As he sailed into the room the boys stood and greeted him.

'So, today, as you are no doubt aware, is the last official time together. Speech day for the junior school this afternoon. We, the upper echelons, will have to wait another day. As always, the best is saved till last. Here before me are the much-awaited English results.'

He began to return them, each warranting a witty remark or affectionate joke. Then the numerical gradings were announced. He did not get much further than Dyson before Down asked, 'Is there any sign of Arthur yet, Father?'

Goddard looked at him. The well-planned tapes seemed to twist and tangle. The commentary of exam results shuddered to a halt. Goddard peered at the boys as if they were total strangers. At last, he gathered some strength from somewhere and forced an answer.

'No news, Dowd—yet.'

'Benjamin wasn't in the dorm last night Father,' said Sackville.

'Yes. He isn't about this morning, either,' added Hardy.

'Perhaps he found Arthur and they're both hiding,' suggested Manning. 'Maybe their results were too terrible, they were afraid of facing ...'

'That's enough,' rasped Goddard, clapping his hands for silence. 'I know where Benji is. In fact, I know where they both are.' He opened Dyson's examination booklet, closed it, and read on through the list until he came to Stanfield. He picked up the booklet to read Benji's stellar essay. His eyes fell upon a red scrawl on the cover.

'Who wrote this filth in this book? Which one of you? Own up. Who is responsible? Very well. He knows who he is. All of you will carry his guilt for him. All of you will write out one hundred times, before lunch, "I must not abuse him who stands between me and Heaven." Begin now.'

Almost spent, Goddard left the room. Most of the boys sat, amazed, while a few of the more reckless scrabbled up to the rostrum to read the filth for themselves. The scrawl read, 'Thou Shalt Not Kill.' in big schoolboy letters.

'What did Benji write that on his answer for?'

'Funny,' mused Sackville, 'it's the first time I ever realised that one of the ten commandments was "filth".'

'If you ask me,' said Dowd, though nobody had, 'he's losing his marbles.'

'Losing them?' said Hardy. 'He lost them years ago. That's why they sent him here—they couldn't get the strait-jacket over his wings.'

'What are we supposed to write?'

'Forget it—all right everyone?' answered Sackville. 'As a group. No one does it.'

'This is all Benji's doing, you know,' said Cawley, 'Benji seems to have finally cracked God.'

> *When shall I, frail man, be pleading*
> *Who for me be interceding*
> *When the just are mercy needing?*

148

> *Righteous judge of retribution*
> *Grant thy gift of absolution*
> *Ere that reckoning days conclusion*

Goddard attended the prize-giving for the junior school that afternoon. He remained outwardly calm, assisting with the endless prizes and handshakes, but one hand never left the worn rosary beads in his pockets, and the constant re-murmuration of prayers kept his lips trembling slightly

When the day was over, he went to find out which priest would be saying the evening Mass. Father Piers was on his way to the sacristy when Goddard intercepted him with an extraordinary request.

'Father, I have just received terrible news. Some old friends of mine have passed away and I was wondering if you could say a Requiem Mass for them this evening. It is very important to me.'

'Of course Father, I will. But surely you would like to say the Mass?'

'No.'

'Father. May I have the names of the departed.'

'No. Just refer to them as ... my little company of friends, please.' Piers made a note of this quaint description of the deceased. 'Another thing, Father. I will not be attending Holy Communion.'

Father Piers stared as Goddard hurried to the chapel.

> *Guilty, now I pour my moaning*
> *All my shame with anguish owning*
> *Spare, Oh God, thy suppliant groaning*

The altar was stripped and a plain white altar-cloth placed upon it. Father Piers wore the stark black chasuble of the Requiem. Goddard had asked Sackville and Hardy to be servers at the altar. No bell rang, no music played, and the sad priest knelt alone at the back of the chapel praying for the repose of the souls of his little company of friends.

> *Now I kneel, with heart submission*
> *See the ashes, my contrition*
> *Help me, in my last condition.*

There, in the quiet darkened chapel he remained, all night, by himself.

'Thou hast no mind for sacrifice or burnt offerings. If I brought them, thou wouldst refuse. Here, Oh God, is my sacrifice, a broken spirit. A heart that is humbled and contrite. Thou, Oh God, will never disdain.'

He beat the Mea Culpa against his heart three times—'Through my fault, through my fault, through my most grievous fault.'

He rose and walked slowly towards the altar—his eyes never left the beautiful triptych of the Betrayal. The fatal kiss on the cheek, the brutal cut of the ear, the gentle healing hand.

> *Ah! That day of tears and mourning*
> *From the dust of earth returning*
> *Men for judgement must prepare him*

'God forgive me,' he cried.

'He will not.' Benjamin's voice echoed round the building, magnified to an ethereal quality. Goddard looked madly about —the voice was coming from everywhere.

'God,' he whispered in terror.

'You have sinned and now you must be punished.'

'Benji? Is that you? God help me ... Benjamin?'

'Good evening, Father. Here I am, watching tenderly over you, watching you suffer.'

Goddard held his head to shut out the haunting voice. His body began to sway rhythmically as if something inside had finally snapped.

'You can't shut me out, you know. My body lies where you left it, cold and decaying. But the spirit is free to watch your lovely suffering. Not in Heaven. Not in Hell. I'm here on Earth.'

Goddard crouched to the ground as if flayed by physical tortures. He moaned.

'Have you thought that I might be in your own head and not real at all? After all, it's not a very sound head, is it? Getting on in years. Confused by jokes and halucinations and murders you can't talk about. Made physically impotent by your vows and morally impotent by your confessional. A Court of Mercy! A Court of Mercy indeed! You don't even know whom your mercy is for, sitting alone on your box, not looking at people.'

'Come to think of it, you don't even know who you're listening to now, do you? Surely you don't think it's Benjamin whose head you so recently battered in with a spade, up there in the woods.'

Goddard looked up. He drew short, painful breaths.

'Oh yes, Father, I know all about that. I actually saw it happen. After all, it was I who engineered everything. And who am I?'

Goddard was aware of another living presence. He looked around desperately seeking the source of the hovering voice.

'I'm the boy you've always detested. The one who never felt your precious mercy.'

A scraping sound came from the ornate stone pulpit. He tried to focus his eyes till he could see quite clearly Arthur Dyson holding the microphone. For a fleeting moment his face became childish and welcoming.

'Arthur. Oh, Arthur, it's you. God be praised, you've come back to life. It's a miracle.'

Arthur smiled malevolently at the stupid remark. He switched off the microphone and let it clatter to the floor.

'Yes. Me. Arthur. But not a miracle. There is nothing supernatural at all about my resurrection. You see Father, I'm a super-mimic. That's all. When you've not got much of a leg to stand on, you soon discover other things to get you through. If you had taken more notice of me you would have realised I am famous in the school for my impersonations. I'm very good at doing you.' He took the slingshot from his blazer pocket. 'Here is another of my equalisers. This is how I killed Charlie —though it wasn't difficult. Your police friends had slowed him down, Benji hit him with a rock—but that didn't kill him.' Arthur produced a stone and drew a bead on Goddard. 'He was crawling across the clearing—just about as far away from me as you are now. I just took aim and—Whamm! Stone to the temple and down he went like a bull in a slaughter house.' Arthur pulled the powerful rubber band and aimed at Goddard.

'You'd kill a priest in his own church?' said the prostrate figure, more incredulous than fearful.

'No, Father. Never. Not when you've got so much to live

for.' Arthur laughed a high chilling laugh. It was almost girlish. He turned abruptly and shot at the face of an angel high above the nave. The nose and one side of its face shattered and fell to the ground. He shook the sling at Goddard like a missionary's crucifix held up to terrified natives in all those 'Fear of God' holy pictures.

'This is my good leg to stand on. The equaliser.'

Goddard said coldly, 'It won't equalise anything with God.'

'GOD!' shouted Arthur. 'If God had wanted to stop me he'd have done so before now. He certainly slowed me down in life.' He tapped the brace with the weapon. He looked up at the faceless angel and giggled. 'Most of what I've done, I've done in his house, under his very nose.'

Goddard moved into a sitting position and shook his head sadly.

'You never suspected, did you? Never for a moment doubted it was Benji in the confessional,' said Arthur in his finest Goddard voice. Then, in his own, 'It was those soft "r" sounds of Benji's that made it so easy. Of course, being invisible to you and speaking in a whisper helped enormously. Remember, you even helped me once. You told me, when I was Benji, not to lean so close to the grille because it distorted the sound.'

'But it was Benjamin who confessed. I know it was.'

'A couple of times, yes, but after that it was me. Listen.' He bent forward and whispered into the priest's ear. The hissed sibilance was cruelly like Benjamin. Goddard listened in total bewilderment as Arthur relived his first triumphant confession.

'I don't understand, I do not understand anything. How could you have done this?'

'How could I? Poor spastic Arthur, so feeble, stupid, tiresome. On the contrary, it's you who've been stupid. Think about it. Nearly everything I've done was within a couple of feet of you. How pathetic you are. How strange you should have been taken in, Father. I thought your order were meant to be specialists in reading people. Your clever, incisive order.'

'Mockery, mockery,' said Goddard bitterly. 'The fume of an evil little heart.'

'Have you looked into your own recently, Goddard?' The priest remained silent, assailed by conflicting emotions. Rage

152

at his fall, shame at his foolishness, and mortification at the
deep tragic condition in which he found himself.

'Perplexed, Father?' chirped Arthur. 'Oh surely a wily old
dog like you is not fooled by such a classic detective-story
device as a man seeming to murder himself. It's very simple.
All I had to do was fix my spare brace and an old school sock
on Blakey's leg. I left it nearly uncovered. I knew you would
assume it was me buried there. Why shouldn't you? Your dear
sweet Benji had confessed it, hadn't he? You always believed
him, didn't you? Actually, that made my job much easier.
Sometimes, it seemed like you wanted it to be him who killed
Charlie.'

Goddard tried to speak, but could not. Arthur chuckled.
A few faint imbecilic sounds sputtered from the priest.

'What, Father, lost your tongue? Lost your mind? Don't
say those cheap tricks of mine with Benji's exercise book
and the Macaulay poems ... I must say, though, it was a
stroke of luck that Benji found you at the grave when he
did. I told him to follow you up there. He was upset that you
were falling to pieces—but he also wanted to see if my trick
was better than his. Father—say something. Where is this
Jesuit fibre we've heard so much about? Give me a boy till
he's seven and I'll make a credulous nincompoop out of him
for the rest of his life.'

'But why?' Words burst out of Goddard like a flood.
'Arthur, why? Why? In God's name, why?'

Arthur eased himself into a pew and said quietly. 'How
strange you can't guess.'

'Guess?'

'Ever since I've been at this school, here in your power,
under your rule—in the Kingdom of Goddard—you have
done nothing but hate and humiliate and punish me without
mercy.'

'No.'

'Yes, yes!' he screamed. 'Every day you found some way to
hurt me.'

'Dear God.'

'Did you know Benji lost his faith? You drove him from
the church. Then you sent him to Hell, Father, to suffer every
torment through all eternity.'

'Is there so much hate in you?'

'No. Only great coldness. There was hate once, when I ached for you to look at me the way you looked at Benji. When I hung on your every word, when all I could talk about was you—what you did, what you said. I needed your love.'

'My—love?'

'Why did you hate me?'

'I didn't hate you ever. I did what I did for your own good.'

'Good!' Arthur began to crumble.

'For your strength. Surely you understand that? What I did to you was stern, I know, but it was for you. I did it from love.'

'You love me,' spat Arthur scornfully, 'that's rich. That's bloody rich. All your love and kindness was reserved for Benji. Tall, popular, handsome, uncrippled, do-no-wrong, sweet-smiling lovely Benji. There was never a crumb of affection for me.'

Goddard got up from the floor and held out his arms to Arthur. 'But there was, Arthur. Believe me, there was. Surely you can't have been that blind?'

Arthur stood and took a faltering step towards him. 'Why did you reject me, Father ...' his voice broke into crippling tears. Goddard took a step towards him and held him in his arms. For the first time he seemed clear-headed and strong.

'I had to choose the stern way. I was your teacher. Finally, I was your confessor.'

Arthur shook himself free and spoke with sudden resolve. 'You were not a very good confessor, Father. You were trapped by the sacrament.'

'You are right, I totally failed its mystery.'

'It failed you, you mean. It is you who have been destroyed.'

'No, my son, it is I who have failed. I never suspected the existence of two personalities on your side of the partition, just as you never suspected the existence of two presences on mine —myself in visible form, and Christ in spirit.' He laughed harshly. 'It's funny—no, ironic—so fitting to think that both of us were representing another essence. Perhaps a better man would have understood and done ... better.'

Arthur limped away from him. The moment of weakness was over. 'A better priest would not have got himself into this mess,' he called, contemptuously, over his shoulder.

'I am no longer a priest. I have forfeited that.' He reached out his hand in a gesture of supplication. 'Two boys have died. We are both in mortal sin. You need all the love and guidance I can give you—as a man, as a friend.'

Arthur turned on him, enraged. 'Of what use is your cold guilty love?'

'It is still love. It is all I have left to give.'

'It's no use to me. You forget, I am dead, absolved of my sins.'

Goddard bowed his head in real agony. 'You don't know what you are saying. My child, you are ill and in great despair. Come, let us pray together. We are both in the same box from now on. We both need to find the way back to reconciliation with God's grace.'

He moved towards the boy, but Arthur darted out of reach with ungainly agility, challenging the priest to catch him.

'Don't run from me. Don't tease me, boy. Don't provoke me. Don't hide from me. We need each other,' he pleaded.

'Keep away from me, God, I hate you like I hated Benji, and both of you I have destroyed.'

'Don't speak like this. Come to me.'

Arthur's eyes glittered and his face became suffused as the madness poured out of him. He crouched like a wild cat at the foot of the altar, spitting out his words.

'Father God, it seems to me you have only two choices. One is to go to the police and tell them you killed Benji, which puts you in prison for life—or rather, since you won't be able to tell them why you did it without violating the seal of the confessional, in a lunatic asylum. Your other choice is to commit suicide, which I need hardly remind you is the most damning of mortal sins. And will put you in Hell for eternity. An intriguing problem for one of your training. If it was up to me, believing what you believe, I think I'd choose detention for life in preference to Hell. It will be more comfortable, and the sentence will be shorter.'

His passion subsided. He gave Goddard a pitying glance, then turned on his heel and limped slowly past the dazed priest into the shadows. Goddard uttered a terrible cry and fell backward onto the floor of the church in a still, stunned, despair.

Arthur, arrested by the cry, remained a long time in the

shadows, watching the fallen man. Shaken by the sound, he approached the prostrate form. For a long moment he looked down at the priest, who looked back up at him with lifeless eyes. He spoke quietly to Arthur.

'I thought you had gone.'

'I am going. I just wanted to take a final look at a fallen god.'

'Where are you going to?'

'I don't know yet.'

'What will you do?'

'Hide. Before the sun comes up I'll be miles away.'

'Hiding from yourself.'

'Yes. No. From other people.'

'Then what? Then where? Tell me.'

Arthur started to cry. The towering victorious dragon-killer was suddenly his own age again. 'I don't know. I don't know. I don't want to be alone anymore.'

Goddard's voice was hard. 'You won't be alone any more wherever you go. You'll be travelling with your murderous sin. It will hang on your back. It will stick closer to you than your own shadow. It will slow you more than that brace.'

'No. I have been absolved. You gave me absolution.'

'Do you really think so? Am I looking at a boy who has a hearty sorrow and detestation of what he has done?'

'Yes. Yes.'

'I think not. In my own intriguing problem, as you call it, I at least have the certainty of forgiveness, but you, with your scalding envies and loathsome pride have a truly dreadful journey to go. I can do nothing for you, so you'd better start now.' Arthur fell to his knees beside him, tears flowing freely.

'Start for where? I have nowhere to go, you know that. I was only pretending I had. Father, I'm frightened. Help me, please, help me.'

Goddard rose to a semi-recumbent position and looked at the shaking boy who mirrored his own agony.

'Can I?' he asked. 'Will you hear me? Will you help yourself? Will you trust me?'

'Trust you! If you'd only known how much I've idolised you over these years. I'd have done anything for you.'

Goddard gently lifted the boy's face and wiped away the tears. Softly he kissed the crown of his head.

'Not for me ... for yourself, and so partake of God's great mercy. My time is done. I am destroyed, but you are in my charge and it must not be so for you. Tomorrow I will inform my superiors. Also I will go to the police. To the police I will confess the murder of both boys, giving some reason that will satisfy—criminally insane, heaven knows, there is enough evidence for that. God, I know, will ease me from the consequent calumny of this world. I will also make arrangements for you with Father Mackkerras. This is my confession to you, and you must faithfully keep the secret. But listen, Arthur, rejoice in it, don't be burdened by this compassion, but pray for me as I will pray for you, that you may learn to become one of his truly illuminating servants.'

'You would do that for me, Father?'

'No. For myself. Forgive me, God, but I am not fit for any glorious martyrdom. I am doing what I am doing for myself. Do you understand that?' Arthur nodded. 'Good. Then let us now pray for those boys, and for ourselves. Do you know the responses of the Litany of the Dead?'

They knelt and faced each other, murmuring the prayers from the Last Agony.

'You saints of God,' the man began.

'Come forth to me,' the boy replied.

'You angels of the Lord
Receive my soul
Eternal rest grant unto me
And let perpetual light shine upon me
Oh Lord, hear my prayer
And let my cry come unto thee'

'Lord have mercy,' said Goddard, and awaited the response. When it did not come, he opened his eyes and looked at Arthur.

Arthur bent across and kissed him on the cheek.

Goddard wept.

Absolution.

In a Trappist monastery overlooking the French Atlantic coast, a man who had served time in prison had grown too old to keep up his silent day of work and prayer. He lived in a cell with very little apart from a bed and a crucifix on the window-sill, and an enigmatic picture of a young Marist Brother in white, carrying a South American Indian boy on his shoulder.

On a bright April morning, a monk who cared for him, saw the familiar white-haired figure bend to pick up something that had slipped from his lap. On going to his assistance, he found a letter card. It simply said, 'Brother Christopher, formerly Arthur Dyson, Doctor of Medicine, was killed in the service of the Lord in South America.' Pinned to it was a small picture—showing the same man whose likeness he kept in his cell. As the monk bent to pick up the letter, he found that his charge was dead. Father Goddard's heart was already limping into heaven.

THE END